"You are ... you for my wife. You cannot believe I want to end our marriage before it has really begun."

The hot sulphur of his glare tinged her tender emotions. "You want out of our marriage. You say so. You do not want to be the mother of my *bambini*. Fine. *Non è problema*. Go."

For the second time she was being told to leave Rico's life. Only this time if she went, would he ever let her back in?

Apparently he truly did want to remain married. Knowing that, could she leave him? *Did she want to leave him?* The answer was simply no.

"I don't want out of our marriage." She whispered the words.

"Then you sleep in my bed."

Lucy Monroe

THE ITALIAN'S SUITABLE WIFE

ITALIAN HUSBANDS

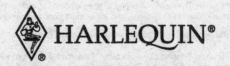

HARLEQUIN®

TORONTO • NEW YORK • LONDON
AMSTERDAM • PARIS • SYDNEY • HAMBURG
STOCKHOLM • ATHENS • TOKYO • MILAN • MADRID
PRAGUE • WARSAW • BUDAPEST • AUCKLAND

To my critique partners, Erin and Kati.
Your friendship is something I will *always* treasure.
Thank you for being in my life and being the
special women *that* you are.

ISBN 0-373-12425-2

THE ITALIAN'S SUITABLE WIFE

First North American Publication 2004.

Copyright © 2004 by Lucy Monroe.

www.eHarlequin.com

Printed in U.S.A.

CHAPTER ONE

His lips hovered above hers.

Would they make contact? They never had before, no matter how much she ached for it. He started to lower his head and her heart kicked up its pace. *Yes. Oh, yes.* This would be the time. But even as she strained toward him, he began to back away. His image dissolved completely as the discordant note of a ringing telephone tugged her toward consciousness.

Gianna Lakewood picked up the cordless handset still half immersed in dreamland, a land where Enrico DiRinaldo was not engaged to supermodel, Chiara Fabrizio.

Her voice still husky from sleep and the emotions elicited by her dream, she said, "Hello?"

"Gianna, there's been an accident." The sound of Andre DiRinaldo's voice brought her eyes wide-open as tension immediately tightened her grip on the phone.

"An accident?" she asked, sitting bolt upright and flipping on the bedside light almost in the same motion.

"*Porco miseria.* How do I say this?" He hesitated while she waited with a premonition of dread for what was to come. "It is Enrico. He is in a coma."

"Where is he?" she demanded, jumping out of bed and clutching the phone to her ear, her green eyes wild with the fear coursing through her. She didn't ask what happened. She could find that out

5

later. She needed to know where Rico was and how soon she could get there. She started shucking out of her pajamas.

"He is in a hospital in New York."

New York? She hadn't even known Rico was in the States, but then she'd avoided news of him since his engagement to Chiara had been announced two months ago.

She hopped over to the nightstand, one leg still encased in cotton pajama bottoms, and grabbed a notepad and pen from the drawer. "Which one?" She wrote it down. "I'll be there as soon as I can!"

She hung up before Andre could say another word. He would understand. He had thought to call her even though it was the middle of the night whereas Rico's parents would have waited until morning in misguided courtesy. Because Rico's brother knew that Gianna had loved Enrico DiRinaldo since she was fifteen years old.

Eight years of unnoticed and unrequited love, even his recent engagement to another woman had not been able to dampen those feelings.

She rushed around her tiny apartment, throwing together the necessary items for her trip to New York. She considered checking into flights, but discarded the idea. It was a two-and-a-half-hour drive, but it would take longer to get to the airport, book a flight and make the plane trip to New York. She wasn't like the DiRinaldos. She couldn't command first class attention, or even hope to get on the next available flight unless an economy seat was vacant.

She didn't bother to take a brush to her chestnut-brown, waist-length hair, leaving it in the braid she slept in. Nor did she take time to throw on makeup.

She barely dressed, leaving off her bra and slipping into a worn pair of jeans, lightweight sweater and tennis shoes, no socks.

A scant two hours later she walked into the hospital and asked to see Rico.

The woman behind the information desk looked up and asked, "Are you family?"

"Yes." She lied without compunction. The DiRinaldos had always said she was family. The only family she had left. The fact she could claim no blood relation was irrelevant at the moment.

The woman nodded. "I'll call an orderly to take you up."

Five minutes that felt like five hours later, a young man dressed in green scrubs came to lead her to ICU. "I'm glad you're here. We called his family in Italy three hours ago," so just before Andre had called her, "and they won't be here for another five to six hours. In cases like this having loved ones around in the first hours can make all the difference."

Well she wasn't a *loved* one, but she loved and she supposed that had to count for something. "What do you mean, cases like this?"

"You know Mr. DiRinaldo is in a coma?"

"Yes."

"Comas are very mysterious things, even with all the medical knowledge we have today. There's a case to be made for the presence of important people in the patient's life bringing him out of the coma." The orderly said this with a certain acidic bite she didn't understand.

They stopped at the nurse's station and she was given instructions for her visit with Rico. She also learned why the *orderly* had seemed so knowledge-able about Rico's condition. He was actually the intern working with the ICU doctor on call.

She walked into the ICU unit, her eyes not taking in the medical paraphernalia surrounding Rico. All she could see was the man in the bed. Six feet four inches of vitality as lifeless as a waxwork doll. Eyelids covered the compelling silver eyes she loved so much. His face was badly bruised and one shoulder was splotched with purple as well.

He didn't appear to be wearing anything but the sheet and blanket, which covered most of his torso. His breathing was so shallow, her heart literally stopped in her chest at first because she thought he wasn't breathing at all.

She moved forward until she stood beside the bed, her lower body pressed against the metal bedrail. Her hand reached out of its own volition to touch him. She desperately needed to feel the life force beating beneath his skin. Seeing no bandages, she laid her hand very lightly over the left side of his chest. Her knees almost buckled with emotion.

The steady beat of his heart under her barely touching fingers was proof that as still as he was, as pale as he looked, Rico was still alive. "I love you, Rico. You can't die. Please. Don't stop fighting."

She didn't realize she was crying until the intern handed her a tissue to wipe at the tears sliding silently down her cheeks. She took it and mopped up without once taking her focus off the man in the bed.

"What happened?" she asked.

"They didn't tell you?"

"I hung up before his brother had the chance.

Getting here seemed more important than getting details,'' she admitted.

"He was shot saving a woman from a mugging."

"He was shot?" The only bandages she saw were on his head.

"It was just a crease—" the orderly pointed at the white gauze strips "—along his cranium, but he fell into oncoming traffic and was hit by a car."

"The bruises?"

"Were from the car."

"Is there any lasting damage?"

"The doctors don't think so, but we won't know until he wakes up."

There was something in his voice and her head snapped around. "Tell me."

"The nature of some of his injuries could result in temporary or permanent paralysis, but there's no way of knowing for sure until he comes out of the coma."

"Where is the doctor?" She wanted more information, more than the opinion of an intern, no matter how knowledgeable he might be.

"He's making rounds. He'll be in to see Mr. DiRinaldo in a little while. You can talk to him then."

She nodded and turned her eyes back on Rico, immediately forgetting the intern was in the small cubicle. There was only Rico. He'd filled her world for so long, the prospect of a life without him in it made the pain she'd felt upon his engagement pale into insignificance.

"You have to wake up, Rico. You have to live. I can't live without you. None of us can. Your mother, your father, your brother…we all need you. Please don't leave us. Don't leave me.'' She even forced herself to mention Chiara and his upcoming wedding. ''You'll be married and on your way to being a papa soon, Rico. I know that is what you want. You always said you were going to have a houseful of children.''

She'd hoped with the naïve dreams of a girl that those babies would be hers, but she didn't care if Chiara was the mother, Gianna just wanted Rico to live. She kept talking, pleading with him to wake up, not to give up and she told him over and over again how much she loved him.

She was holding Rico's hand and willing him to come out of the coma when the doctor came by later.

He examined Rico's chart and checked the electronic monitors by the bed. ''All his vital signs look good.''

''Isn't there anything you can do to wake him up?'' she asked, her throat raw from swallowing tears.

The doctor shook his head. ''I'm sorry. We've already tried stimulants to no effect.''

Her hand tightened on Rico's unmoving one. ''I guess he'll just have to wake up on his own then. He will, you know. Rico's got more stubborn genes than a Missouri mule.''

The doctor smiled, his tired blue eyes warming a little. ''I'm sure you're right. It's my opinion, having family around does its part, too.'' His tone was censorious, but she didn't feel it was directed at her.

''His parents and brother will be here as soon as humanly possible. It's a long flight from Milan, even on the fastest private jet in the world.''

"I'm sure you are right. It's too bad his fiancée couldn't see her way to staying."

"Chiara is here, in New York?"

"Miss Fabrizio was contacted at her hotel. She came in and became hysterical at the sight of him, furious he'd risked his life for *a woman too stupid to know not to walk alone at night.*" This time the censure was blatant.

"But why isn't she here?" Perhaps Chiara had stepped out to use the facilities or something.

"She stayed for about an hour, but when we informed her he was in a coma and we didn't know how soon he'd come out of it, she decided to leave. She left a number to call when he *wakes up.*" There was a wealth of disgust in his words.

"She must be really upset." Gianna looked again at Rico's motionless countenance and had no trouble understanding his fiancée going to pieces over it. She couldn't imagine leaving his side, but then everyone dealt with fear in their own way.

"She'll sleep fine tonight. She insisted we prescribe her an oral sedative," the doctor added.

Gianna nodded absently, once again focused almost entirely on Rico. She rubbed the skin of his hand with her thumb. "He's so warm. It's hard to believe he isn't sleeping normally."

The doctor made some comments about physiological differences between coma and normal sleep that she only half listened to.

"Is it all right if I stay?" she asked, knowing it would take an orderly for each arm and one for her legs to get her to move from Rico's bedside.

Laughter rumbled in the doctor's throat. "If I said no?"

"I'd sneak back in wearing scrubs and a mask and hide under the bed," she admitted, amazed she could find any humor in a hospital room with Rico lying broken in the bed.

"As I thought. Are you his sister?" the doctor asked.

She felt the blood rush into her cheeks. Should she lie again? Looking at the understanding light in the doctor's eyes, she didn't think she would have to. "No, I'm a family friend."

Speculation flickered briefly in his expression before he nodded. "I won't tell if you won't. It's obvious you care. Your presence can't hurt and may very well help enormously."

Relief swirled through her bloodstream. "Thank you."

"It's all about what's best for the patient." The doctor exited the cubicle thinking it was a pity his patient wasn't engaged to the tiny woman who obviously cared so much instead of the gorgeous Amazon with a heart like a rock.

Gianna was only vaguely aware of the doctor's departure as memories of Rico assailed her. She picked up his hand. It was heavy and she kissed his palm before laying it back on the bed, her own covering it.

"Do you remember the year Mama died? I was five and you were thirteen. You should have hated having me tag after you. Andre called me a pest often enough, but you didn't. You held my hand and talked to me about Mama. You took me to Duomo Cathedral, such a beautiful place, and told me I could be close to Mama there. It hurt so much and I was scared, but you comforted me."

She suppressed the memory of how different it had been a year ago when her dad died. Rico had been dating Chiara then and the other woman had no time for Gianna and had made sure Rico didn't, either.

"Rico, I don't want comforting now. Do you hear me? I want you to get better. I thought nothing could hurt more than when you announced your engagement...but I was wrong. If you die, I don't want to go on living. Do you hear me, Rico?" She leaned forward, her head resting against the strong muscles of his forearm. "Please, don't die," she pleaded as tears once again bathed her skin and his.

She was dozing when a familiar voice repeating her name woke her up.

"Gianna? Wake up, *piccola mia*."

She lifted her head from its resting place by Rico's thigh. Sometime in the last five hours, she had lowered the bedrail and settled her head beside him. She needed the physical contact as a reminder that Rico was still alive.

Her eyes slowly focused as she blinked in the subdued lighting of the ICU cubicle. "Andre, where are your parents?"

He grimaced. "They left only two days ago on a cruise aboard a friend's yacht to celebrate their anniversary. Papa insisted on complete privacy and secrecy. They won't be back for another month and I know of no way to contact them. Rico was the only one with that information."

He left unsaid the obvious. Rico was in no condition to share his knowledge with them. Her insides twisted when she thought of the reaction Rico's parents would have to the news of their son's accident and Andre's inability to reach them.

"If he dies…" Andre's emotion-filled voice trailed off.

She glared at the younger version of Rico. "He won't die. I won't let him," she said fiercely.

Andre reached out and squeezed her shoulder, but said nothing. He didn't need to. They both knew she could not will Rico to live, but that wouldn't stop her from trying.

"The doctor said there has been no change in his condition since it stabilized after he was brought in."

"Yes." She'd been there for every blood pressure check, every time a nurse came in and read his monitors, marking the stats down on his chart.

"When did you arrive?" he asked.

She shrugged. "A couple of hours after you called."

"The drive is longer than that."

She just looked at him and he sighed. "It's a good thing you didn't get a ticket. Rico would have blasted you for it."

"When he comes out of his coma he can lecture me all he likes about my driving."

Andre nodded. "I know." Then his gaze skirted the room as if looking for something. "Where's Chiara? I thought she was supposed to be with him on this trip. She's modeling in some show while Rico attends the banking conference."

She told him what the doctor had said and Andre cursed eloquently in Italian, then switched to Arabic when he saw the way her face turned red. "I'm sorry. She's just such a bitch and my brother's too smitten to see it."

The image of a love-struck Rico was both painful and funny. "I can't quite imagine Rico's judgment completely obliterated by a pretty face, Andre. I'm sure there are things about Chiara that he genuinely admires. He's marrying her after all. He must love her." Even saying the words hurt, but she gritted her teeth against the pain of acknowledging Rico's desire for another woman.

Andre snorted. "More likely he's sexually obsessed with her. She knows how to use her body to its best advantage."

If her face had been red before, now it was flaming. "I…"

Andre sighed. "You are so innocent, *piccola*."

She didn't want to dwell on her twenty-three-year-old virginal status. She'd never wanted any man but Rico and he'd never seen her as anything other than a younger sister.

"How was your flight?"

Andre shook his head. "I don't know. I spent the entire time praying and worrying."

She reached out and gripped his hand, never letting go of her connection with the man in the bed. "He'll be all right, Andre. He has to."

"Have you eaten since you got here?"

"I haven't been hungry."

"It's hours past breakfast," he admonished her.

And that was how the next four days went. Rico was moved to a private room, per Andre's instructions. Gianna took the opportunity to shower. Other than that, she refused to leave Rico's room. She spent every moment, waking and dozing, by Rico's bedside. Andre bullied her into eating and drinking only by bringing the food and beverages into Rico's room.

Chiara came to see Rico once a day and stayed for five minutes each time. She looked at Gianna with a mixture of scorn and pity. "Do you really think this incessant vigil will make the least difference? He'll wake up when he wakes up and then he will want me by his side."

Gianna didn't bother to argue. No doubt Chiara was right, but it didn't matter.

It was three in the morning on the fifth day. The hospital halls were quiet, the nurse had taken Rico's vitals at midnight and no staff had come to disturb the silence of his room since. Andre was asleep on a reclining chair in the corner. Gianna couldn't doze, so she was talking again and touching Rico.

She brushed his arm and looked lovingly into his still face. "I love you, Rico. More than my own life. Please wake up. I don't care if it's to marry Chiara and give her all the babies I want to have. I don't care if you kick me out of your life after hearing what a besotted fool I've been the last five days. Just wake up."

She said the last on a note of desperation and was hoping so fiercely for him to make some sign he'd heard that when he moved, she thought she'd imagined it. The muscles of his arms spasmed and his head jerked from side to side.

She pressed the call button while shouting to Andre. "He's coming out of it! Andre, wake up!"

Andre came out of the chair fully alert. After that, everything was a blur. The nurse came running in. Soon she was followed by a doctor and then another nurse. Andre and Gianna were shooed out of the room. Then came the waiting. Gianna paced while Andre first sat and then stood, then paced, then sat again. Finally, the doctor came into the waiting room.

It was the same one who'd been on call the night Rico had been brought in. He smiled at Andre and Gianna. "He's awake, but he's a little disoriented. You can see him for five minutes one at a time."

Andre went first. He came back to the waiting room, his expression troubled.

She was desperate to see Rico and would have brushed by Andre without a word, but his hand snaked out and grabbed her. "Wait, *cara*. There is something I must tell you."

"What is it?"

Andre swallowed convulsively and then met her gaze head-on. The look of anguish in his eyes terrified her.

"What's wrong? He hasn't gone back into a coma, has he?"

"No. He…" Andre took a deep breath and let it out. "He can't move his legs."

CHAPTER TWO

RICO'S eyes were fixed on the doorway when Gianna walked in. She couldn't miss the expression of disappointment that clouded his expression briefly before he masked it.

"Hello, *piccola mia*. Did Andre ask you to come and keep him company waiting for me to wake up?"

The endearment did things to her heart when Rico said it that didn't happen when Andre called her his little one. She smiled, her relief that he was talking so acute, she couldn't get a word past the blockage in her throat for several seconds. She stopped beside the bed, noticing someone had raised the guardrail.

"I couldn't have been kept away," she said with more honesty than was probably wise.

One corner of his mouth tipped up. "Always the nurturer. I still remember the cat..."

His words trailed off. He looked tired. Exhausted, really. "He turned out to be a lovely pet."

"So Mama thought. She gave him the run of the place until he died," he replied, speaking of a tabby cat she had rescued from the road after it had been injured when she was ten.

"Pamela was furious with me and wanted to call the animal people to come take it away," she said, speaking of her stepmother. Gianna smiled. "You wouldn't let her."

"What kind of cat do you have now?"

She'd always had pets, usually strays picked up

18

from somewhere, but once there had been a puppy
her parents had given her when she was four. He'd
been a wonderful friend and she'd cried buckets
when he died. "I don't have any animals."

His face registered surprise. "That's not like
you."

It wasn't by choice. She lived in campus housing
and pets weren't allowed. She had no intention of
burdening Rico with her problems, however. So she
just smiled again and shrugged.

"You haven't asked how I'm feeling."

She gripped the bedrail to stop herself from touching him. She'd gotten so used to the freedom over
the past five days. "You look like you've been pum-
meled on the playground by the school bully. I don't
imagine you feel much better."

That made him chuckle and she rejoiced in the
sound. Then he sobered. "My legs don't move." His
expression and voice had gone blank.

She couldn't resist the urge to take his hand.
"They will. You've got to be patient. You've had a
terrible experience. Your body is still in shock."

His eyes remained unreadable, but his hand returned her grip with betraying fierceness. "Where is
Chiara?"

Oh, Heavens. Gianna had forgotten to call the
other woman. She felt guilty color stain her cheeks.
"I was so excited you'd come out of coma, I forgot
to call." She reluctantly pulled her hand from his.
"I'll do it right away."

"Tell her to come round in the morning." His
eyes closed. "I'll be more myself then."

"All right." She moved toward the door. "Sleep
well, *caro*," she whispered. The endearment was so

common it was like saying *hey you*, but she said it with a surfeit of emotion she prayed he could not hear.

He didn't reply.

Rico waited impatiently for Chiara to come. Andre and Gianna had both been in to see him again this morning and stayed until he had tired. Gianna looked exhausted and thinner than he remembered. He wondered if her job as an assistant professor was taking too much out of her. He'd have to talk to his mother about it.

But even exhausted, Gianna exuded an innocent sensuality that he'd never been completely able to ignore. At times it had made him feel guilty because his body reacted even though his mind saw her as more sister than woman. Regardless of his body's baffling response, he'd never once considered pursuing it. He didn't bed virgins and until recently, marriage had held no appeal.

His damn legs still wouldn't move and the doctors could not tell him if the paralysis was permanent or not. Gianna was convinced it was temporary and had said so again that morning. She was such a sweet little thing. He was surprised she wasn't married yet. She'd be twenty-four next year, but then American women married later, he thought. It was too bad Andre didn't see her as marriage material. Rico wouldn't mind having her in the family.

A surge of something dark and inexplicable stabbed him at the image of Andre walking down the aisle with Gianna. He tried to convince himself it was because Rico didn't know if he would be able to walk down the aisle with Chiara when the time came.

He could very well still be in a wheelchair. But something ugly had shifted in him at the thought of Gianna married.

Was he such an egoist he couldn't stand the thought of losing her innocent adoration? The thought did not sit well.

"*Caro!* You mustn't glare like that. You'll scare the nurses off and then who will bring you your lunch?" A trill of laughter accompanied Chiara into the room.

He watched his beautiful fiancée's entrance. Any man would be proud to claim Chiara for his own, but she belonged to Rico. "Give me a kiss and I won't feel like frowning any more."

She made a moue with her mouth. "Naughty man. You're sick."

"So kiss me and make it better," he taunted.

Something flickered in her eyes but she came forward and offered her lips for a brief salute. He wanted to demand more, but he allowed her to step back from the bed.

"You weren't here last night," he said.

Her eyes filled with tears and her expression was wounded. "That brother of yours and the *little paragon*," she must have meant Gianna, "they kept me out of it. They didn't call me for hours after you woke up."

Why hadn't his brother called Chiara right away? "They were here. You were not."

The tears spilled over. "That horrible girl! She's infatuated with you. She wouldn't leave your side. There wasn't even room for me next to the bed. Half the staff are convinced *she's* your fiancée."

He couldn't imagine Gianna doing something so cruel. "You're exaggerating."

Chiara spun away and her shoulders shook with misery. "I'm not."

"Come here, *bella*."

She turned around and returned to stand by the bed, her face wet with tears. "She lied to get into your room the first night. She told them she was related to you. And she never left, just like some pathetic clinging vine."

"Everyone was upset."

"But I'm your fiancée. I want you to tell her to stop acting like she is and not to spend so much time here at the hospital. I don't want to be tripping over her."

"Are you jealous?" he asked, the thought not unpleasant considering the state of his body.

She pouted with expert effect. "Maybe, a little."

"I'll talk to her," he promised.

Gianna walked into Rico's room an hour after she'd woken from the first unbroken stretch of sleep she'd had in six nights. Andre had insisted she take the other bedroom in his suite, saying it was just going to waste until his parents could arrive. She'd been grateful as her budget did not stretch to Manhattan hotel prices or taxi fares from a less expensive part of the city. She hadn't relished the thought of sleeping in her car or depleting her small savings account to nothing.

Rico looked up, his smile of greeting conspicuous in its shortness.

She stopped a few feet from the bed. "You look

better." And he did. His skin wasn't so pale under the tan and his eyes were clearer.

"Gianna, we need to talk."

He'd found out how she had refused to leave his side. He knew she loved him and he pitied her.

She swallowed the knot of pain her pride had lodged in her throat. "Yes?"

"You are like a sister to me."

She hid the pain those words caused, but remained silent.

"You care about my health and this is understandable, but *cara*, you must not push Chiara aside in your concern for me."

He thought she'd pushed his fiancée to the side? Gianna wanted to defend herself, but to do so would require telling him Chiara hadn't wanted to be with Rico when he was so sick. She couldn't do it. It would hurt him too much when he was vulnerable from his injuries.

"I didn't mean to push her aside," she said instead.

"I did not think you did. You are too tenderhearted to deliberately hurt someone like that, but you must be more considerate in future, no?"

She nodded, choking on the words she wanted to say. "I'll try," she promised.

"Chiara does not want you visiting so often," Rico went on.

"What do you want, Rico?" she asked helplessly.

"I want my fiancée to be happy. This is a trying time for her. I do not want her upset further."

It was a trying time for him too, but Rico never considered his own needs. He thought only of protecting those he loved. "Andre said you refuse to contact your parents."

"There is no need for them to cut short their holiday."

"Your mother would want to be here."

"I do not want to be fussed over." The impatience in his voice made her smile.

"I'm surprised you're not working."

"*San celio.* Andre refused to bring in the laptop and the doctor ordered the phone removed when he found me talking to our office in Milan last night."

"What time last night?" she asked, pretty sure she knew the answer.

"What time do you think? When the office opened."

Which would have been roughly 3:00 a.m. No wonder the doctor had the phone removed. She shook her head. "You are supposed to be resting. How can you get better if you won't let your body recuperate?"

"What choice have I?" he demanded, indicating his still legs below the blanket.

She took several involuntary steps forward until she was next to the bed. She laid her small hand across his large one. "You don't have any choice right now, but you will get better."

His silver gaze caught hers and his hand turned until their fingers were entwined. "*Cara*, you always believe the best, no?"

She nodded, unable to speak. The feel of his hand holding hers was such a sweet torment she didn't want words to intrude.

"I believe the best also. I will walk again." He

said it with such arrogance, how could she help believing him?

"When have you merely walked, Rico?" she asked with a husky voice she did not recognize.

His free hand came up and cupped her cheek and a look she did not understand passed across his face. She went completely still, allowing every fiber of her being to absorb the delicious feeling produced by his touch. It would be gone all too soon and she didn't want to waste a moment of it.

His eyes narrowed. "Chiara believes you are infatuated with me, *cara.*"

"I…" She swallowed.

"I told her you are like my *sorello piccola.*"

Like his little sister? Yes, she knew he saw her that way, but she did not look on him as a big brother and her senses were running riot with his hand on her cheek and his fingers entwined with hers. "Right."

He brushed his thumb across her lips and she shivered.

Silver eyes turned gunmetal gray. "You are cold?"

"No," she whispered. Why was he touching her like this?

"What is going on in here?" Chiara's voice raised in furious censure, broke the spell of Rico's touch and Gianna jumped back.

She forgot her hand linked with his and was pulled up like a dog at the end of its leash as his hold on her did not lessen.

She tugged against her hand, but Rico didn't let go. He was looking at Chiara, his expression unreadable. "I am visiting with Gianna. She is not too busy to spend more than five minutes in my company."

Two things became apparent to Gianna at once. Chiara was jealous and Rico knew it.

"I've spoken to Gianna about letting you take your rightful place at my side, but you must be here to do so, *bella*."

Chiara's beautiful face turned red with temper and she glared at their entwined hands. "I am on assignment. You know I cannot spend every waking moment at the hospital like your pet limpet."

"She has her own job. Yet she finds the time."

He hadn't even bothered to protest the *pet limpet* remark, so she did it. She yanked on her hand. Hard. He let go. "I'm no one's pet, Chiara. I'm a friend and I didn't realize my visiting Rico would upset you so much."

Chiara's glare did not lessen. "You expect me to believe that, the way you've carried on for the last week. Andre treats me with contempt and you, he insists on keeping in his own suite at the hotel."

"You are staying with Andre?" Rico demanded, a tone in his voice that sounded very much like disapproval.

"There are two bedrooms in the suite. I'm using one until your parents arrive."

"They aren't coming."

"Because you won't call them," she said with some exasperation.

He ignored that. "It is not seemly for you to stay with an unmarried man alone in his hotel suite."

"It would be even less seemly for me to sleep in my car."

"*Per favore*, spare us the dramatics," Chiara jeered.

Gianna wanted to smack the beautifully painted red lips, but she wasn't a violent person…at least she never had been. She supposed there was a first time for everything. "Where I stay is neither of your business," she said firmly.

Chiara's eyes shot disdain at Gianna. "It is when you take advantage of the generosity of my fiancé's family to keep yourself underfoot and in the way."

"Stop playing the shrew and come here. I want my kiss of greeting," Rico demanded of Chiara.

He hadn't bothered to deny she was in the way and for all Gianna knew, he felt the same as his fiancée. He'd told her not to visit him as much. But he had taken Chiara to task for being rude. That was something at least.

Still, perhaps it was time for Gianna to go back to Massachusetts. She hadn't had her position long enough to accrue significant vacation time and since she wasn't related to Rico by blood, the university administration did not see her absence as a family emergency. The department head had already made one not very veiled threat regarding her job if she wasn't in class teaching the following Monday.

Chiara was obeying Rico with an overkill of enthusiasm. Gianna turned to give the couple some privacy, but the kiss lasted minutes. Finally, the pain of being in the room with the man she loved while he kissed another woman got to her and she walked out, sure they wouldn't notice.

"I told you she had a crush on you." Chiara's voice floated out the open door and down the hallway to where Gianna waited for the elevator.

Gianna felt waves of mortified color sweep up her skin. She'd spent eight years nursing a secret love and to have it laid bare for that witch to mock was more than she could bear. She was furious with Rico too. He'd used her to make his barracuda of a fiancée jealous. All that touching that had meant so much to her had been nothing more than a ploy to keep Chiara in line.

Evidently Rico didn't approve of his fiancée's flying visits any more than Gianna and Andre did.

"Gianna's feelings for me are of no concern to you." Rico could hear the bite in his voice and did nothing to mitigate it.

Chiara's kiss had not blinded him to her vicious attitude toward Gianna, an attitude he would not tolerate. "And you will not speak to her again as you did when you arrived. Her genuine concern for me is not something to mock."

Chiara's eyes widened in shock. "How can you say these things? Another woman's feelings toward you are definitely my concern."

"Gianna is no threat to you." But even as he said the words, he wondered at their truth. Would he have kissed the younger woman if Chiara had not arrived when she did? He didn't like to believe he was capable of such a dishonorable act. His affections were committed to Chiara, but he hadn't wanted to let go of Gianna's hand and the feel of her soft lips under his fingertips had caught at his emotions in a way Chiara's extended kiss had not.

"She's a little schemer and it devastates me that you can't see that." The tears welling in his fiancée's eyes did not move him as they once would have done.

She'd spent too little time at his bedside and her complaints about Gianna simply did not ring true. He wondered just who the schemer in this situation really was.

Gianna waited until the following evening to visit Rico again.

He was talking on a hospital phone and typing on a laptop set up on a desk across his legs when she came in. She smiled wryly to herself. Nothing and no one could keep Rico out of business circulation for long. He looked up and spotted her. He motioned to a chair near the bed and she sat down, waiting patiently for him to finish his call.

Lines around his eyes made him look tired, but he had more color and his jet black hair had been washed and styled in its usual neat fashion. He wore a navy-blue silk pajama jacket that looked brand new. It probably was. She didn't imagine Rico was the type of man to wear pajamas to bed.

He rang off and moved the desk with the portable computer aside. ''Been busy sightseeing?'' he asked with an edge to his voice.

''Sightseeing?'' she asked incredulously.

''You have not been in to see me since yesterday morning.''

He needn't sound so accusing. ''You said Chiara didn't like me visiting so much.''

''I did not mean for you to stop coming all together.'' Silver eyes snapped their disapproval at her. ''For all you knew I had slipped back into a coma.''

He was being totally unreasonable and for some

reason she found that terribly endearing. It was almost as if he'd missed her. "I'm here now," she said soothingly, "and Andre would have told me if you'd taken a turn for the worse."

"*Si*. Andre, whom you share your hotel room with."

"We don't share a room." She examined his face for a clue to the source of his irritability. "Are you in pain?"

He glared at her. "I have been shot and hit by a car driven by a man who could not see his hand in front of his face in a brightly lit room. Of course I have some pain."

He sounded so outraged, she had to stifle a grin. "I don't think the driver was expecting a man to fall in the street in front of him."

Rico dismissed that with a flick of his hand. "Blind fool," he muttered.

"Andre said you saved the woman's life. They caught the mugger and he had a list of prior offenses as long as your arm, most of them were violent assault and he'd already killed two women." Andre had also told her that the woman had come by the hospital to thank Rico, but he had told his security to keep out all visitors except her, his brother and Chiara. "You wouldn't let her thank you."

"I do not need this thanks. I am a man. I could not drive by and do nothing."

"If you ask me, you're more than an average man." She smiled at him, letting him see her approval. "You're a hero."

His eyes warmed slightly. "Chiara believes all this," he indicated his unmoving legs, "is my fault."

Gianna jumped up and laid her hand protectively

on his arm. "No. You mustn't think that. You were being the best kind of man. You paid a price, but you wouldn't let that stop you from doing it again."

His hand came up to hold hers and she was reminded of the day before, both of the wonderful feelings his touch invoked and the way she'd felt used when she realized he'd touched her only to make Chiara jealous.

She pulled her hand away and stepped back. "I don't plan to stay long," she said quickly, lest he think she was clinging like the limpet Chiara had accused her of being.

"Why? Do you have a hot date with Andre?" he asked scathingly, his unreasonable anger back in full force.

"He's taking me to dinner, but I'd hardly call it a hot date."

"Do not pin your spinsterish hopes on my brother. He is not ready to settle down."

She clenched her teeth. "I'm not pinning anything on him, much less a desire to marry. We're going to dinner because *he* doesn't mind my company."

"I do not mind your company." He pointed at his chest with an arrogant finger. "You could have dinner here, with me."

"What's the matter, can't Chiara get away from her busy modeling schedule to share a meal with you?" Gianna asked with uncharacteristic bite, still stinging from the way he had used her to make the other woman jealous the day before.

His remark about spinsterish hopes had done nothing to make her feel more charitable toward him, either.

His look could have stripped paint. "My fiancée is none of your business."

Gianna's heart melted. It had been a rotten thing to say and she just knew all that anger was hiding pain. Chiara was a totally selfish person who wouldn't know how to put herself out for another human being if her life depended on it. Worse, here was Rico, tired, in pain, not sure if he'd walk again and Gianna doing her best to act like a witch as well.

"I could call Andre and ask him to pick up dinner and bring it here," she offered by way of a peace offering.

"I will call him." And he did just that. He made arrangements with Andre in a burst of staccato Italian before hanging up the phone.

"I told him to get you your own room."

"I heard you, but it won't be necessary. I'll only be staying one more night. Surely my reputation and his virtue will be able to survive such a short test."

Rico looked disgruntled. "I did not say you would attack him."

"How else would a spinster like me expect to get a macho Italian male like your brother to the altar?"

"Why do you say you will only be staying one more night?" he asked, sidestepping her taunting words.

"I'm going home tomorrow."

"Why would you do this? I am not well. Do you see me ready to leave this place?" He sounded like a man ready to explode.

She couldn't imagine why. "You don't need me to stay and hold your hand. You've got Andre and Chiara. And your fiancée doesn't like having me underfoot." The words still rankled.

"You did not remain by my bedside for five solid days for Chiara's sake."

So, he knew about her vigil. Probably realized how much she loved him, too, which was all the more reason for her to leave. Her pride had already been dented but good by Chiara's nasty comments.

"You're better now."

He reached out and grabbed her wrist, pulling her close to the bed. His expression was intense, the hold on her wrist almost bruising. "I am not well. I am not walking."

"But you will walk."

Frustration was apparent in the set of his firm lips. "Yes. You believe this. I believe this, but my brother, my fiancée, they have their doubts."

"You'll just have to prove them wrong."

He nodded, heartwarming in his arrogant confidence of his return to full health. "I do not wish to do this alone."

Such an admission from Rico was astonishing and she couldn't gather her wits enough to respond.

"I need you here, believing in me, *cara.*"

She almost fainted, she was so shocked at his words. "You need me?" she asked in a choked whisper.

"Stay." It sounded more like an arrogant command than a plea for her support, but Gianna knew what it had cost him to say it and she could not refuse.

"Okay."

He smiled and pulled her close for a kiss of gratitude.

At least that's what she assumed it was supposed to be, but Rico kissed her lips, not her cheek and the moment their mouths connected, their surroundings ceased to exist for her.

CHAPTER THREE

COLORS in every hue swirled around her as Gianna's lips tasted Rico's for the first time. His mouth was firm, warm and tasted faintly spicy. She inhaled and was engulfed in his masculine scent. *Rico.* She ached to run her fingers through his hair, to explore the contours of his chest under the pajama jacket. She probably would have, if he didn't have such a firm hold on her wrist.

Her other hand was gripping the bedrail with white-knuckle intensity.

He broke the kiss and she hung there, suspended in a world of sensation she was not ready to leave. Her eyes opened slowly to see him smiling at her.

"Thank you."

"Thank you?" For what? For kissing him?

"For staying," he replied, not without some amusement.

And it hit her. It *had* been a kiss of gratitude. Here she was, poised to reconnect with his lips and he was smiling at her like an indulgent older brother, pleased he'd gotten his own way. She straightened and spun away so quickly the long braid down her back arced over her shoulder to land against her left breast. "N-no problem. I'll call the college and let them know I won't be returning right away."

She had a feeling that phone call wouldn't go over very well, but even if it meant losing her job, she wouldn't leave Rico. Not as long as he needed her.

Andre arrived with dinner and Rico ate the beautifully prepared pasta dishes and steamed vegetables with fervor. "This is a great improvement over the food served here."

"You could have your meals delivered," Andre replied.

Rico shrugged. "It has not been my main concern."

No, Gianna thought, that would be reserved for business and walking again. Maybe even in that order.

"Something that does concern me is Gianna staying in your hotel room. I do not like this."

Andre gave his brother an interested appraisal. "Why not?"

"It is not good for her reputation."

Gianna couldn't help laughing at this. "Rico, you're a total throwback. No one cares if I stay in Andre's suite."

"I care," Rico informed her with an attitude that said that was all that should matter.

"Well, *you* are not my keeper. I haven't got the money for a prolonged stay in a hotel room." Particularly if she lost her job.

"I will pay for it."

She glared at him. "No, you will not."

"Besides, there is no need," Andre inserted. "My suite has two bedrooms and since you won't call Papa and Mama back from their cruise, the second one will go empty if Gianna does not stay in it."

She thought Andre's argument had merit. From the angry tilt to Rico's chin, he did not agree.

He pinned her with a look that sent shivers to places she had yet to discover. "You will allow

Andre to care for your needs, but you refuse my help?''

She barely suppressed the urge to roll her eyes. ''It's not the same thing. It doesn't cost Andre anything more to give me the extra room in the suite.''

''You think I begrudge you this trifling amount?'' Rico demanded.

Why was he being so obtuse? ''No. Of course, not. It's simply that I'm already there.'' She laid aside her fork and allowed herself to make direct visual contact for the first time in an hour. She'd perfected the art of talking to his shoulder since almost making a complete fool of herself over that kiss.

''I don't know what you're so worried about, Rico. My name doesn't make it into the social columns on a regular basis. No one cares where I sleep or who I do it with for that matter.''

His expression turned feral and she found herself scooting to the back of her chair, her body posed stiffly away from him.

''You have shared your bed with a man?''

Heat scorched up her cheeks until they burned like the Chicago fire of 1908. ''That's none of your business.''

''I do not agree.'' He looked ready to get up out of the bed and shake an answer out of her.

Even knowing that was not possible did not suppress the shiver of apprehension that skittered down her spine. She swung her gaze to Andre, appealing to him for help with her eyes, but he was obviously enjoying the conversation too much to step in on her behalf. She looked back at Rico.

His expression had not softened at all.

''I really don't want to talk about this with you.''

"You will tell me the name of the man."

Heavens. When had her silence become an affirmative answer? And what right did he have to grill her like this? If Chiara were still a virgin, Gianna would dance naked on the top floor of the Empire State Building. "Are you saying you and Chiara don't sleep together?"

"This is not under discussion."

"Nothing is under discussion," she came close to shrieking.

"You are very red. You are embarrassed, no?"

Why bother denying it? He'd know she was lying. Her blush had already given her away. "Yes."

"A woman of experience would not be so discomfited," he said with smug assurance.

That set her over the edge. "Are you sure about that? Maybe I've slept with tons of men. Maybe I'm even sharing Andre's bed now and the two room suite is only a ruse."

She realized she'd let her temper lead her into deep, dark waters a second before he exploded. Mr. Cool Italian business magnate sent the portable table with his dinner on it careening across the room and started shouting at Andre.

Gianna spoke fluent Italian, but she didn't recognize some of the words. From the ones she did, she guessed they were curses. Andre's usually smiling face was stiff with shock. He tried to tell Rico it was a joke, but Rico's fury did not abate. His hands pounded the air, punctuating his angry speech and if he had been mobile, his brother would have been flat on his back. She was sure of it.

"For Heaven's sake." She jumped out of her chair and crossed to the bed, standing between Rico and

Andre. "*Calm down.* I said what if, not that I had. Rico—"

His arms snapped around her waist and she found herself sitting next to him on the bed, her chin cradled in a surprisingly gentle but firm hold. "Do you sleep with my brother?"

"No. I've never been with any man," she admitted, thinking nothing but the truth could completely diffuse the situation.

Rico's glare was sulfuric. "Yet you taunted me with the idea you had."

She couldn't begin to understand why it mattered so much to him. Perhaps he felt responsible for her in some way since her father had died. She wouldn't have known it by the way he'd ignored her for the past year, but maybe the feeling was there all the same.

"I wasn't taunting you. You embarrassed me and made me angry. Most women are not...not..." She couldn't make herself say the word. "Well, by my age, most women have some experience."

"But you do not."

"I do not." She agreed and stifled a depressed sigh. With him marrying Chiara, that wasn't likely to change, either.

He brushed her cheek with his fingers before dropping his hand from her face. "You should not be embarrassed to speak of these things to me."

She didn't know where he'd got that from. How could she help but be embarrassed to talk about it? She'd never even admitted her lack of practical application when discussing the subject with her girlfriends in college. But she didn't want to spark another outburst so she remained silent.

She went to get up, but his arm around her waist prevented her. "Rico?"

"You are very innocent."

She grimaced. That had been well and truly established. "If you're finished dissecting my lack of a love life, could I get up please? I want to go back to the hotel."

His hand was warm against her waist and he was idly brushing his thumb back and forth in a manner guaranteed to drive her mad or into a lustful frenzy. She wasn't sure there was much difference between the two.

"You will move to another room."

"No." Andre's firm denial surprised her into looking at him, regardless of the fascination Rico's small caresses held for her.

Andre's face was set in hard lines. "This is New York, Enrico. It would be inadvisable to allow Gianna to stay in a room by herself, even in a hotel with security."

"Then I will assign one of my security people to watch her room."

This conversation was growing more bizarre by the minute.

Andre shook his head in a short, decisive negative. "How can it be better for her to stay in a hotel room with a stranger than with me?"

Her attention swiveled back to Rico. He was scowling thoughtfully. "Perhaps we should get Chiara to stay in the suite as well."

"No!" Andre and Gianna chorused at once.

Rico's brows rose. "What bothers you about this?"

How did you tell a man you could not stand his

fiancée for dirt? Gianna cleared her throat, trying to think of a tactful way of putting her absolute refusal to share living space with the selfish witch.

"Gianna told me what Chiara said about her," Andre said, disapproval clear in his voice. "Your fiancée's unfounded jealousy was the reason Gianna considered going back to Massachusetts in the first place."

"Now you seek to protect her from my fiancée?" Rico asked with silky vitriol. "Are you sure there is nothing you two wish to share with me?"

She'd had about enough of Rico's overdeveloped sense of responsibility toward her. She was not some helpless female in need of his protection. She'd been on her own, if not physically then emotionally since long before her father had died. Or maybe Rico really thought she'd set her sights on marriage to the younger DiRinaldo brother.

"This is ridiculous. I'm not about to trip Andre and try to beat him to the floor."

Andre smiled, all Italian male. "Which is not to say, *cara,* that I will not be so inclined."

The hand on her waist tightened and Rico glared retribution at his brother. "Your humor is misplaced."

"So is your hand, considering you are engaged to marry someone else," Andre taunted.

Rico's hold did not loosen one bit. "She is practically family."

"Is she?" Andre asked. "I wonder."

"*What I am* is tired of this conversation." She yanked on Rico's hand at her waist. He let go and she stood up.

Setting both fists on her hips, she directed her next

words to Rico. "If you want me to stay in New York, it will be in Andre's suite and Chiara's services as chaperone will not be required. Even virginal spinsters have their standards and mine don't run to primitive, arrogant males who talk about me as if I'm not even in the room."

Rico winced at the word spinster and Andre's expression turned calculating. "It is true, Enrico is almost medieval in his outlook, but I am a modern man. I do not see anything wrong with a twenty-three-year-old woman remaining unmarried."

"Fine, *modern man*, take me back to the hotel. I'm ready for some of my own company."

Rico grumbled some more about her staying in Andre's suite, but in the end he acquiesced. He didn't have any choice. Gianna loved him enough to risk her job, but that didn't make her a doormat.

Doormat was the last thing Rico would have called Gianna over the next two weeks. She harangued him about working too much and not participating in his physical therapy sessions enough. She argued when he had the fast modem line installed in his room at the private hospital he'd moved to. That same day he had caught her unplugging the phone beside his bed and giving it to an orderly to take away. She'd been unrepentant.

Whereas Chiara spent very little time at the hospital and refused to attend his sessions at all. She'd left for Paris two days before to model in a Fall fashion show. Which was fine by him. No man wanted his woman around to see him helpless and that's how he felt with his damned useless legs refusing to do what he wanted them to.

If a part of him was relieved to see the back of his fiancée and her nagging comments about Gianna, who could blame him. He'd made her angry more than once defending the younger woman and was sure to do so again. He would not allow anyone to denigrate the girl he'd spent a good portion of his life protecting...even from himself. Chiara's attitude regarding his health had also worn thin. She said she believed he would walk again, but her eyes said not.

Gianna was not so reticent. She continued in her unwavering belief that feeling would return to his lower body in due course. She reminded him repeatedly that spinal shock injuries often resulted in complete recovery given enough time, something one of the doctors had asserted the first week. She also not only attended the physical therapy sessions, she participated in them. Which he did not thank her for. He needed her belief in him, not her interference.

"Get me back my phone," he gritted at her.

She shook her head, her long chestnut braid swinging gently from side to side catching the light and his attention. What would the richly colored hair look like unbraided? It was easily long enough to fall past her waist. Did she ever let it down? It would be beautiful.

"That was the third call in fifteen minutes." Gianna frowned at him like a diminutive schoolteacher lecturing a student caught passing notes in class. "You aren't going to walk again talking on the phone."

The physical therapist had the gall to nod his agreement. "Gianna is right, Mr. DiRinaldo. You need to concentrate on your therapy."

The therapist smiled conspiratorially with Gianna

and Rico's blood pressure climbed several notches. The overmuscled, blond Adonis was supposed to be the best physical therapist in New York, but Rico would gladly have flattened him.

"You wouldn't take a phone call in the middle of negotiating an important deal, would you?" Gianna asked.

"I am not negotiating. I am sitting here bored out of my skull while he," Rico pointed to the therapist with one hand, "moves my legs as if that will magically make them start working on their own."

"It's not magic. It's work and I wouldn't have thought you were afraid of hard work," she jeered.

"*Porco miseria!* I, Rico DiRinaldo, afraid to work? You are out of your mind."

"Good. I'm glad you said so." Her pixie chin set at a stubborn angle. "Then you understand why the phone is not allowed for the rest of the session."

"At least let me forward it to my answering service." Once she got back the phone, he could finish his call and *then* he would unplug it if she was so insistent.

She crossed her arms, pressing surprisingly feminine curves for such a small woman into prominence. "I already did it. You're not getting the phone back, you might as well accept it."

He gave her the look that sent bank presidents running for cover, but she just stood there, arms crossed and did not budge.

He turned to the therapist. "Give me something to do."

The other man jumped at the tone of his voice and Rico felt a small measure of satisfaction that unlike Gianna, the therapist found him intimidating.

*   *   *

Gianna knocked lightly on Rico's door, but heard no answering voice within.

She'd made it her habit to arrive after breakfast and stay through the morning's physical therapy. Perhaps Rico had already been taken down to the treatment room. She was running a bit late. She had overslept. The day before had been exhausting and ended in a late night.

She'd driven to Massachusetts and back all in one day so she could retrieve her belongings from the furnished university apartment that was no longer hers. Her prediction the department head would not see her staying in New York in an understanding light had been right on. But she'd finally found something to be grateful for in the debacle following her father's death.

When her stepmother had sold the house, Pamela had tossed everything she did not want to keep personally. Which meant that Gianna's belongings fit in her car and she would not have to go to the expense of renting a storage facility.

When there was no answer to Gianna's second knock, she pushed the door open. She wouldn't mind missing his session. They were getting more and more difficult for her to handle. The therapist insisted on Rico dressing in sports shorts and a body hugging T-shirt for his physical therapy. Every ripple of Rico's muscles was visible to her obsessive scrutiny.

She felt like a voyeur watching him exercise his incredibly gorgeous body.

It would be fine if she could encourage him and be the unaffected "cheerleader" on the inside she portrayed on the outside, but she wasn't. She had

loved Rico since she was fifteen years old and
wanted him almost as long. Apparently temporary
paralysis and a foul temper were no deterrent to those
feelings. She felt like some kind of depraved sex
fiend.

The sight that met her eyes when she came into
the room stopped her like a clanging train crossing.
Rico sat on the side of his bed, wearing nothing but
the sexiest pair of briefs she'd ever seen. Not that
her untried eyes had seen all that many, but it
wouldn't have mattered if she'd seen a thousand men
in their skivvies. This was Rico.

He was the only man that mattered.

She practically swallowed her tongue trying to
speak. "I... You... The door..."

His head swiveled round and the look on his face
was a revelation. He looked elated.

"Rico? What..."

"You are having a difficult time with your sen-
tences, *cara*."

She nodded mutely.

His mouth curved in a wide grin and his eyes glittered silver triumph. "I can feel my toes."

It took a second for the words to register, but when
they did she flew across the room to hug him. She
landed against his chest with all the momentum of a
dead-on run. Rico went backward and she went with
him, her arms wrapped around his neck, her mouth
babbling her excitement.

"I knew it! I knew you could do it!"

His hard male body shook with joyous laughter
under her. "And is it I, *piccola mia,* that has done
this or *il buon dio?*"

Laughter trilled out of her to mingle with his. "A

bit of both, I think." She grinned down at him.
"When did it happen?"

"I woke before dawn with a tingling in my feet.
The tingle became feeling as the morning advanced."

The satisfaction mingled with relief in his voice
tugged at her emotions and her heart just melted.
"Oh, Rico..."

"Do not turn into a waterworks on me, woman."

Her smile was misty, but she managed to blink
back any real tears. "I wouldn't dream of it. I'm just
so happy," she said in her own defense. Then she
did something she would never have done had she
been thinking clearly. She kissed him.

It was just a small salute on his chin, but her lips
didn't want to move once they landed against Rico's
warm, stubble covered jaw. She wanted to go on
kissing him, tasting his skin, nibbling at his neck.
She knew she had to move away, but she couldn't
do it. She told herself she would let it last just one
more second and then she would get off him and let
him get dressed.

Then it hit her. Where she was. What she was
doing. Rico was barely dressed and she was plastered
all over him like a sticky blanket. She reared up,
which had the effect of pressing her legs in a V over
his thigh and pushing her skirt up at an indecent angle. She tried to get her knees under her to crawl off
of him, but only managed to put her body into intimate contact with male flesh for the first time in her
life.

It paralyzed her.

The thin silk of her panties were no barrier to the
heat of his flesh and the erotic stimulation of his

hairy leg between hers. She should have worn tights today instead of her short boots and slouchy socks. At least then her thighs would not be bare against him. She felt a flush crawl up her body from her toes to her hairline. The heat was caused by both embarrassment and physical pleasure. "Rico... I..."

"You have lost your words again, *piccola mia.*" Lazy amusement laced his voice.

She felt like anything but a little girl at that moment. In fact, she'd never felt more like a woman. "I'm sorry," she muttered as she once again tried to move away from him, but two very strong hands at her waist held her still.

"You have nothing with which to reproach yourself. Your excitement equals my own."

She doubted it. Where his excitement was limited to a very natural joy at the prospect of walking again, hers had a large dose of sexual awareness mixed in. The hands at her waist moved and she found her face directly above Rico's.

"I am happy, *cara.*"

"Me, too." She tried to control her breathing, but pulling air into her lungs had become an Olympic event.

His mouth quirked. "I could tell."

"Could you?" she asked stupidly, her mind focused on the ten different ways she wanted to close the gap between his mouth and hers.

Silver eyes flared wide and primal man came to the surface as Rico became aware of her preoccupation.

"Have many men kissed that luscious bow of a mouth?"

"W-what?" Had he just asked her if she'd done

much kissing? She couldn't take it in. Rico had no reason to be interested in her kissing history.

Her thoughts cut off midstream as Rico went about discovering her level of experience for himself. Though she was on top, she felt as if his lips were drawing hers, holding her captive with masculine domination of the most basic kind.

She felt a hand at the back of her head, holding her in place. She could have told him it wasn't necessary...if she could stop kissing him long enough to speak.

His lips molded hers with expert precision and she found hers parted without having been aware of opening them. His tongue ran along her lips before dipping inside her mouth, sharing an intimate sort of kiss that had disgusted her in the past. With Rico, she found it exciting beyond belief and she squirmed against him like a wanton.

Her hands explored his naked chest with abandoned delight while her tongue dueled shyly with his male aggressiveness. Soon, the entire world was reduced to his body under hers, his mouth against her mouth and their mingled breath.

''Rico!'' The feminine shriek from the doorway brought Gianna out of her sensual haze with shattering speed.

CHAPTER FOUR

GIANNA tore her mouth from Rico's and rolled aside as his hands fell away from her. She jumped off the bed and straightened her short plaid wool skirt while her skin crawled with embarrassment to match the cherry-red of her ribbed turtleneck sweater.

"You filthy little slut," Chiara raged at her while Rico pushed himself back into a sitting position.

Rico rapped out something in Italian, but Gianna's senses were still so fogged up she didn't catch anything but his comment that he hadn't expected Chiara back in New York so soon. Whatever else he said, it caused Chiara to reel back like a drunken sailor and then glare at Gianna with undisguised malice.

Chiara stormed over to the bed, her high heels clicking on the floor, her eyes promising murder and mayhem. "That is obvious. I won't tolerate this sort of thing, Rico! Do you hear me?"

Gianna thought the entire medical staff probably heard her, but forbore saying so.

Just before reaching the bed, Chiara swung to face Gianna. "Do you think I don't know what was happening? I am not so stupid I believe Rico made a play for a plain little thing like you. It is obvious you were throwing yourself at him in some desperate attempt to get him to notice you as a woman, but you will never be enough woman for a man like Rico...even paralyzed."

Each word found their target in Gianna's vulnerable heart. She knew she wasn't Rico's type. Never had been. And she felt guilty because she knew Chiara was right. Gianna had thrown herself at Rico, kissing him, going all gooey-eyed on him when all he'd been doing was sharing his good news.

Of course, none of that explained why he'd kissed her back. But then with a man of Rico's machismo, maybe the reaction was automatic.

She opened her mouth to apologize, when Chiara spun away and addressed Rico. "You either send that wretched girl away, or I'm leaving and I won't come back."

Everything inside Gianna froze. Given a choice like that she knew what decision Rico would make. Hadn't he made it time and again over the past year when Chiara had made sure he had nothing to do with Gianna, even to the point of dragging Rico from Gianna's father's funeral with indecent haste?

"Well, Rico?" Chiara demanded, her full, glossy lips set in a pout, her eyes filled with crocodile tears that made Gianna grind her teeth.

"I think you know my answer," Rico replied.

They were the last words to register as Gianna spun and walked as fast as her wobbly legs could carry her from the room, real tears burning a path down her cheeks.

She thought she heard Rico call her name, but she dismissed the idea as fancy.

He'd made his choice.

He would send her away, but as of yesterday, she officially had nowhere to go. Which did not lacerate her heart with near the effectiveness as the fact Chiara had successfully evicted Gianna from Rico's life.

*   *   *

Gianna plopped down onto her bed in the hotel suite, grateful Andre was at a banker's meeting in Rome on Rico's behalf. She could do her packing and grieving in private.

She felt like she had when her father died: alone, lost and in pain. And humiliated. Though, humiliation was something she hadn't felt at her dad's death. The memory of her shameful reaction to being on top of Rico mortified her. How could she have been so brazen? Rico probably thought she was some kind of nymphomaniac virgin.

She groaned and buried her face in the bedspread covered pillow. Hiding her face did not hide her tormenting thoughts. She'd made an absolute fool of herself and she felt sick to her soul acknowledging it. The phone rang, but she ignored it to wallow in her misery. It was probably just housekeeping or something.

Or maybe one of Rico's doctors. Darn it. She forced herself to sit up and reached for the phone just as it stopped ringing. She couldn't work up any real chagrin she'd missed the call. She didn't want to talk to anyone right now.

But thinking the caller might have been one of Rico's doctors introduced another line of thinking to add to her misery. With her gone, who was going to make sure Rico focused on his rehabilitation? The therapist, big blond giant that he was, was afraid of Rico. Even Andre hesitated to cross his brother in Rico's current mood. Andre had been the one to arrange for the high-speed phone line to be installed in Rico's room at the hospital.

No one would be around to make sure Rico didn't

channel too much of his energy into business instead of getting better.

Tears burned the back of her eyes. She'd been such a fool and because of it, Rico would suffer. She wasn't so arrogant she thought he really needed *her*...but he needed someone to help him stay on track and Chiara certainly wasn't going to do it. The beautiful model was too self-centered to care.

Gianna curled into a fetal position and concentrated on not letting the tears fall.

She didn't know how long she wallowed in her gloomy despair, but she eventually got up and started packing. The sound of the door opening in the outer room alerted her to Andre's return. She hadn't expected him back from the banking conference until tomorrow. She'd have to face him sometime and tell him about her stupidity and Chiara's ultimatum. It might as well be now.

She trudged into the living room of the suite only to stop and rub her eyes, sure they were playing tricks on her.

"Why did you not answer the phone?" Rico raked at her, his face set in furious lines.

"I didn't know it was you," she said rather stupidly.

He was here. In the suite. Other than the streamlined wheelchair, he looked every ounce the powerful Italian businessman. His dark hair gleamed smoothly against his head and his Armani suit was immaculate.

More intimidating than that was the incandescent fury gleaming in his silver eyes. "You ran away."

"I thought you wanted me to go." His fiancée certainly had. "Where's Chiara?"

His mouth set in a grim line. "Gone."

"Because of me?" she asked, stricken to the heart at the thought her shameless behavior was to blame for Rico losing the woman he loved.

"Because I do not allow others to dictate my friendships."

Gianna bit her lower lip until she tasted blood. "I'm sorry I jumped on you like that."

"You were excited about my news. So was I."

"But I..." She swallowed and screwed up her courage to say it. "I kissed you."

"That is not the way I remember it, *tesoro mio.*"

"I acted like a...a hussy. I attacked you," she said miserably.

"You behaved like a warm and vibrant woman when confronted with the unexpected physical proximity of a man you are attracted to." He rolled the wheelchair forward. "You are attracted to me, no?"

Her hands curled into fists at her side in an effort not to reach out and touch him. "Yes."

She ducked her head, breaking eye contact with him. She did not want to see the disgust he was bound to be feeling at her admission to being attracted to a man engaged to marry another woman.

Warm, masculine fingers touched her chin, lifting her head. "This is nothing for you to be ashamed of, *cara.*"

"But, Chiara..."

"Is gone." The words sounded very final.

"You mean she's not coming back? Didn't you tell her it meant nothing? She knew I was to blame already."

"She does not wish to tie herself to a cripple."

Gianna felt the words like a blow and she dropped to her knees by Rico's feet. She grabbed his hands and held them to her breast. "You are not a cripple. It's just temporary. Doesn't she realize that? Did you tell her you felt your toes this morning?"

Rico's expression blanked. "What I told her is of no concern to you. She is no longer in the picture. Accept it as I have."

"I..." She felt so guilty, but what could she say?

He turned his head and looked through the open door to her bedroom. The suitcase on the side of the bed told its own story. "You were going to leave, no?" Strangely enough, he sounded angrier by her supposed defection than Chiara's.

"I thought that was what you wanted," she repeated.

"It is not. Did I not say I wanted you to stay?"

"Yes, but—"

"There is no but. You stay with me." *Mother,* he sounded arrogant.

"I—"

"You will not return to the university to teach. You promised me this."

"I couldn't go back if I wanted to," she admitted wryly, "they fired me."

She suddenly realized where she had his hands. She might as well be mauling him again. Dropping them with the speed of a lightning bolt, she jumped to her feet. His fingers curled possessively around her wrist before she could move away. He tugged until she found herself on top of Rico for the second time that day, but this time in his lap. She ended up sitting sideways to him, her legs dangling over one hard muscled thigh.

"You were fired?" he asked, his silver gaze probing hers.

"Yes. So, I'm footloose and fancy-free." She tried to smile about her lack of a job or any prospects in that direction. Getting an assistant professorship right out of university had been a fluke she couldn't expect to repeat. "I can stay with you as long as you need."

"What of Pamela?"

The mention of her stepmother's name did nothing to soothe Gianna's agitated feelings. Pamela had made it very clear after the death of Gianna's father that she did not consider their tie familial or binding. "She sold the house and pretty much everything in it and moved away two months after Dad's death. She's cruising the French Riviera with one of my father's former students."

Rico's eyes darkened. "She sold your home? She disposed of your family possessions?" He sounded incensed. He would be, of course. An Italian as traditional as Rico would find it impossible to understand the willful dismantling of the family home and all it represented. The DiRinaldos had been living in the same villa in Milan for over a century.

"Where have you been living?"

She was finding it increasingly difficult to concentrate while sitting in such close proximity to him. "What? Oh, in a furnished flat provided by the university."

"A furnished flat." His mouth twisted with distaste. "How long have they given you to move?" He caught on quick.

She grimaced. "I went up yesterday and packed everything into my car."

"You are homeless?" He made it sound like she was living under a bridge.

"I'm not. I'm staying here for now, but I'll find a

place when you're back on your feet—'' she meant that literally ''—and no longer require my services as cheerleader.''

''This is not acceptable.''

She smiled. ''Don't let it worry you. I'm a big girl. I can take care of myself. I've been doing it since I was eighteen and went away to college. Pamela never wanted me to move home, even for the summers.''

''No wonder you spent vacations with Papa and Mama.''

''Your parents are wonderful people, Rico.''

''*Sì.* Yes, but I think you are also very special.'' His praise warmed her heart and made her smile again.

''Thank you. I think you're pretty special yourself.''

''Special enough to marry?''

Her heart stopped beating and then resumed at supersonic speed. ''M-married?'' she squeaked.

''Perhaps, like Chiara, you do not wish to link your life with that of a cripple.''

Sheer rage filled her at his repeated use of the ugly word and she slammed her fist against his chest. ''Don't you dare use that word to describe yourself! Even if you remained paralyzed for the rest of your life and we both know you won't, you would never be a cripple!''

''If you believe this, then marry me.''

''But you don't want to marry me!''

''I want children. Mama is expecting a daughter-in-law. I think she will like you in that role, no?''

The thought of having Rico's children left her weak, but... ''This is ridiculous. You're angry with

Chiara, but you don't want to spend the rest of your life with me as your wife and you know it.''

"I want to go back to Italy. I want you to come with me.''

"Of course, I'll come. You don't have to marry me to convince me to return with you.''

"And to have my children? Are you content to do that outside of wedlock?''

She could feel her cheeks literally drench with color. "I don't know what you are saying.''

"I'm saying I want *bambini*. Is this so difficult to understand?''

No. It wasn't. Rico would be an incredible father and had never made any secret of his desire to become one. "But...''

"You will have to undergo an IVF procedure. I cannot perform...'' It was his turn to let his voice trail off and she knew it shattered his pride to say the words.

"Of course not. That's only to be expected, but it won't last,'' she tried to reassure him.

His expression told her she had fallen short of the mark.

The forbidden flirted at the edges of her consciousness. It was irrational. It was insane, but for just a moment she let herself picture what it would be like to be Rico's wife. To belong to him and to bear his child. It was all too easy to imagine herself round with his baby...and very, very happy to be in that condition.

"Perhaps you are afraid of the procedure.''

"No.'' She looked at him and sucked in air in response to the intense will beating at her. "Rico—''

He cut her off with a finger over her lips.

"Consider it."

She nodded her head, mute. Even if she hadn't wanted to marry Rico more than she wanted anything else out of life, she would not have refused him flat out. After Chiara's rejection, such an action would be cruel.

"And while you are considering, think of this."

His lips replaced his finger and her brain short-circuited. Zinging electric charges shot from one part of her body to another. Her nipples beaded almost painfully against the silk confines of her bra and an ache of emptiness pulsed between her thighs. This was no kiss of discovery. It was an all out assault on her senses and when Rico's tongue demanded entry into her mouth, she gave it without a murmur.

The pulse in the heart of her womanhood increased its beat, tapping out a message of need she had never before felt.

She moaned and pressed herself against him, her fingers curled tightly around the lapel of his jacket. His hand tunneled under her sweater and caressed the vulnerable skin between her shoulder blades, making her shudder. Then she felt the clasp of her bra give and a masculine hand cupping the fullness of her breast. Shocked delight froze her. She'd never allowed any of her dates to explore and had never had a hand on her bra-covered breast, not to mention her naked flesh.

But this was Rico and she craved his touch. She cried out, the sound lost in his mouth as his fingers gently pinched and pulled her nipple into even more aching rigidity. The throb between her legs increased until she felt like screaming. She squirmed in his lap, unable to control the impulse to move.

He pulled his mouth from hers and she chased it with her lips. *He couldn't stop kissing her. Not now.* He didn't. He simply moved from her mouth to the sensitive spot behind her left ear. She shivered. She quaked. She moaned.

All the while his hand kept tormenting her breast while his lips wreaked havoc with her nape.

"You taste so sweet, *tesoro mio.*" Then he proved his words by tasting every inch of skin his lips could reach. The neck-high collar on her turtleneck sweater seemed to get in his way and he tugged at the hem. "Take this off."

Her eyes opened and she stared at him, confused. "What?"

But he didn't answer. He was already sliding the soft red knit up her torso. Her skin tingled where he touched it and she was naked from the waist up before she came out of the passionate daze he'd sent her into enough to realize what he had done. She blinked down at the plush carpet and the small pile of red knit and silk thrown there by his insistent hands.

The silk thing was her bra. She was completely uncovered—open to Rico's hot stare. And it was hot. His silver eyes looked like molten metal as they centered on her now blushing breasts. Her hands flew to cover the vulnerable curves. "You shouldn't look at me like that."

He did not shift his gaze, but gently curled his fingers around each of her wrists, brushing the undersides of her breasts in the process. She nearly came out of her skin at the contact and choked out some kind of inarticulate plea.

"Let me look."

"But…"

His head tilted up and he pinned her in place with his look. "You want me to see."

That was just too arrogant for words. "I don't."

"You do, *cara mia*. It excites you to have my eyes on your flesh, to let me see what you hide from others."

She shook her head, denying it—but knowing he spoke the truth. He could have been touching her, she was so impacted by his stare. He tugged at her wrists and she allowed him to pull her hands away. Then sat there blushing hotly while he looked his fill.

She'd never sunbathed topless, so her skin was pale, contrasting starkly with the reddened, excited flesh peaking each breast.

One long masculine finger reached out and touched the end of a hardened peak. "*Bella…*" he said with a reverence that brought moisture to her eyes. "*Bella mia,*" he added, his tone possessive as both his hands cupped her, one reaching around her ribcage from behind so she felt completely surrounded by him.

She quivered.

He molded her with his hands, gently squeezing, caressing her with an expertise of which she refused to consider the source. She watched in fascination as his head lowered. He closed his lips around her nipple. The sight of his mouth against her untouched flesh sent shards of excitement slicing through her.

Then everything went out of focus.

The feeling was so electric, she could have powered a small town with her excitement. He nipped at her and then soothed the small stabs of pleasure filled pain with his tongue. Her eyes slid shut and her head fell back, her chest heaving with sobs of pleasure. She cried out, ''Please, Rico, please!''

She didn't know what she was asking for. But she needed something. Her body felt on fire. She could not concentrate. She was going to fly apart, explode like a bomb on a very short fuse. And Rico's touch was that fuse—his mouth the match to light it. How could it be anything else? She had dreamed of this moment for almost a decade and her fantasies had never come close to the reality.

In all the world, she had only ever loved this man.

Husky male laughter greeted her desperate pleas while one hand trailed up the inside of her calf. He tickled the back of her knee, making her squirm and then brushed the inside of her thigh. Her legs parted of their own volition and his touch continued its upward journey until he brushed the apex of her womanhood. She jolted with sensation and cried out. He brushed her through the silk of her panties again and she moaned, shamelessly pressing herself into his exploring fingers.

His thumb slid past the elastic band at her leg and touched her intimately, making her whimper with both pleasure and feminine fear. She had never done this. Had never, ever even considered allowing another man to touch her like Rico was doing. In some ways she was more naïve than an adolescent. ''What are you doing to me?'' she whispered.

''Loving you...''

The words sounded so good. She could pretend for just this moment in time that he really did love her, that his touch was spurred by his need for her. The sweet thought increased her pleasure to the point of mindlessness. For right now…Rico loved her as she loved him. If only in her mind.

He pulled her to stand beside him. *Was he done?* The thought sent distressed need coursing through her.

He unzipped her skirt and let the red and black plaid wool drop to the carpet. Then he pushed her silk panties that matched her bra down her thighs. They dropped to pool at her feet. "Step out of them," he commanded her.

She obeyed mindlessly, toeing off her short boots and socks at the same time, wanting nothing more than to return to the safe haven of his lap. She had her wish almost instantly as he pulled her back into his arms and began again with the ministrations to her oversensitized flesh. He probed her warm depths with one finger while his thumb played a gentle sonata on her most sensitive spot.

The sobs returned. The shaking increased. Her body caught fire of the volcanic kind. She felt on the verge of a precipice, desperately wanting to jump off but terrified of what would happen when she did.

"Let go, *cara mia.*" He moved his mouth to her lips, kissing her with passion she had only ever dreamed of feeling. "Give me the gift of your pleasure."

She went over the edge into starbursts and earthquakes. The pleasure went on and on while she screamed and cried, begging him to stop, begging him to go on. He touched her until her body's convulsions almost tipped her off his lap. His hold on her torso was too tight. His touch was too much.

She tried to say it, but no coherent words would leave her mouth and she found herself shuddering in a series of climaxes that left her spent and barely conscious in his arms. He tucked her up against him and guided the wheelchair into her bedroom. He rolled up to her bed and pulled back the covers before lifting her gently onto the cool white sheets. He tucked the blankets around her.

"Sleep, *tesoro*. We will talk tomorrow."

Gianna woke sometime before dawn, the feel of the bedclothes against her naked flesh an unfamiliar one. It only took a few seconds for the events of the day before to come flooding back. Heat traveled up her body as she remembered what she had allowed Rico to do to her. He'd touched her every intimate place. He'd made her scream with pleasure and beg with abandon. And he hadn't even taken off his suit coat.

Why had he done it? Until yesterday, Rico had never so much as noticed she was a woman—except maybe of the sisterly variety. Now, all of the sudden, he'd made love to her with a passionate expertise that had left her nearly comatose. Okay, so they hadn't technically had intercourse, but she wasn't sure she could feel more intimately touched. He'd been inside of her, with his hand.

Just remembering the way he had dominated her body with pleasure had her breath sawing in and out and her heart beating an arrhythmic pattern. It had been a fantasy fulfillment so spectacular that she could live on the memories for the rest of her life.

But she didn't have to, an insidious voice reminded her. He'd said he wanted to marry her. If she agreed, he would not withdraw the offer, even if he wanted to. He had too much Old World honor to even consider it.

He couldn't really want to marry her though. Chiara had rejected him and he had responded with typical DiRinaldo action. He'd asked another woman to marry him and made love to her so incredibly well, her response had to have boosted his male ego. Rico was a macho man and being ditched by the beautiful but shallow Chiara would have left him feeling the need to prove that in some way.

Well, he'd done it.

He'd completely convinced Gianna that his machismo rating was off the Richter scale. Of course, she'd never been in any doubt. Just walking into a room with him in it bombarded her with enough testosterone to set her female hormones raging.

She hesitantly touched the places of her body that still felt achy from his attention. They felt no different than normal…no more or less feminine than they ever had washing those bits in the bath. And yet she felt different. Infinitely more womanly.

Rico had given her that gift—he had made her feel like a complete woman.

The least she could do would be to give him the gift of her understanding in return. She would not use his emotional reaction yesterday to trap him into a marriage he could not possibly want in the cold light of a new day.

She ruthlessly crushed the glowing dreams of being his wife and carrying his child. She would get up and shower and get to the hospital first thing so she could let Rico off the hook before he had too much time worrying about it.

CHAPTER FIVE

GIANNA dressed more carefully for her visit to Rico than usual. She dithered between wearing a doeskin skirt and short jacket set and a long denim skirt with black raw-silk long sleeve T-shirt. The doeskin skirt was short, hitting her right above the knees and even with tights—she felt exposed. She pulled it off and slid into the other outfit before brushing her hair into a large black oval clip at her nape.

She didn't know if her clothes would be sufficient armor against memories of Rico holding her naked body and making her sob with pleasure. She hated the idea of facing him at all, but she refused to be a coward. Yesterday would have to be dealt with and then they could move on. Of course, the less said about the embarrassing episode the better, in her opinion.

This time when she knocked on his door at the private hospital, she did it loudly and waited for him to call for her to enter. She pushed open the door to his room, which resembled Andre's suite at the hotel more than a hospital. Rico was sitting at his desk, wearing the skimpy shorts and form-fitting T-shirt that were de rigueur for his therapy sessions.

His concentration was on the computer, not her, so she took the time to compose herself in the face of his sexy attire. It didn't do much good. She wanted desperately to fall on him and beg for more of what he'd given her yesterday.

The urge left her feeling shaky and she moved to a chair to sit down. "Good morning, Rico. I see you're already at work."

He turned his chair to face her. "*Buona mattina, bella mia.* Did you sleep well?"

And that quickly she felt her composure slipping to the wayside. "Yes," she answered in a strangled tone.

"You were exhausted when I left you."

Her gaze flew to his and she read smug satisfaction in the silver depths.

"You made sure of it."

His smile was all conquering male. "There can be no doubt I will satisfy your needs in marriage, *tesoro.*"

Rico had needed to prove his manliness to himself and he'd done it. One part of her hurt that she'd been little more than another form of therapy for a man frustrated by his limitations. Another part of her— the part that loved him—rejoiced in the fact she could give him back a small part of his pride by admitting her reaction to his touch.

Still, she had never questioned her level of satisfaction married to him. "But you won't be happy, Rico. You don't want to marry me."

"You said this yesterday, but I proved differently, no?"

What did she say to this? She had no desire to tromp on his male ego by telling him she thought he had needed to prove something to himself. On the other hand, how could he seriously contemplate marrying her when only yesterday morning he had still been engaged to Chiara?

"Chiara will come back, Rico. She was angry, but

she'll realize her mistake and you don't want to be tied to another woman when she does.''

His expression hardened. ''It is over with Chiara. I said this already.''

And he didn't like repeating himself.

''But—''

''Do not argue. You want to marry me.''

She gasped at his arrogant claim. ''Says who?''

''I say.''

''It wasn't so long ago you were using me to make your inattentive fiancée jealous.'' Or had he forgotten that bit?

His eyes registered genuine surprise. ''This I did not do.''

He'd never lied to her before and she couldn't tolerate him doing so now, even for the sake of his pride. ''You did.''

''When did I do this?''

''You touched me that day and you knew she would see. I'm not even sure yesterday morning's kiss wasn't for her benefit,'' she admitted, getting the worst of her fears out in the open.

''I have only ever touched you because it is what I wanted to do, *mi tesoro*. How can you believe otherwise? Am I a scoundrel that I would use you in such a way?''

Put like that, she had to pause. His expression said she'd really offended him.

His hand sliced through the air. ''I do not deny her initial jealousy at your attentiveness did not please me, but I have never courted such a thing. I, Rico DiRinaldo, do not need to do such a thing.''

Great. Now she'd offended not only his sense of integrity, but his pride as well.

It did not help her equilibrium that the gesture drew her attention to his sculpted muscles. Weren't only weight lifters supposed to have that kind of definition? "Do you lift weights?"

"What is this?"

Her face burned when she realized what she'd said and she dragged her attention back up his body to the amused expression on his face. "Never mind. It's not important."

"This is true. We have other things to discuss. Will you be disappointed not to have a big wedding?"

"It doesn't matter." She wouldn't care if they got married in the register's office if she believed Rico really wanted to marry her.

"Good. I want to marry before we return to Italy."

"I haven't said I'll marry you." She should not even be considering it. "Look, if this is about what you said yesterday. You don't need to worry. I knew you weren't serious at the time. You were distraught."

"I, Rico DiRinaldo, do not get distraught. This is an emotion for old women and young girls."

What about young women? She was fast approaching that state. "My point is, I'm not holding you to what you said yesterday."

"But I am holding you, *cara.*"

The image of him doing so interrupted her normal thought pattern for several seconds.

He smiled at her as if he knew what she was thinking. He probably did, the fiend.

"What are you holding me to?" she asked, quite proud of herself for remembering the thread of conversation.

"You let me make love to you. That implies a certain commitment. I am holding you to that commitment."

He was devious and too smart for his own good.

She didn't even attempt to say they hadn't made love, because for all intents and purposes they had.

"Women make love with men all the time without marrying them," she said instead.

"Not you."

She glared at him, wanting to wipe that look of overconfidence right off his face. "Maybe I do."

He laughed and she wanted to scream. "You have already admitted your untouched state to me. You cannot prevaricate now."

"Just because I haven't had sex does not mean I've never let a man touch me," she pointed out.

How had she forgotten his unreasonable fury when she'd taunted him similarly before? One second, his chair was several feet across the room and the next he was in front of her, his hands clamped around her shoulders. The hold was not painful, but it was unyielding all the same. "Tell me the truth," he bit out, each word a sharp bullet.

"Why are you so angry?" she asked, feeling helpless in the face of such an irrational reaction.

"You ask this after yesterday?"

Funny, but somehow she had seen the day before as happening to her only. Sure Rico had made it happen, but she hadn't thought of it affecting him in any way. Apparently, giving a woman her first orgasm, or several of them, made a guy feel possessive.

"I've never let another man touch me like you did," she admitted grudgingly. She wasn't about to deal with another eruption like the other day when first she, then Andre had goaded Rico.

His hold changed to a caress on her upper arms. "I believed this. Do not tease me again."

"You're so bossy."

"It comes with being the oldest."

"You'd be that way if you were the youngest of six children," she postulated.

He shrugged, clearly dismissing the subject. "The doctors say there is no problem with returning home within the week."

"What about your therapy?"

"I have arranged for an eminent therapist to treat me in our home in Milan."

There he went, assuming her agreement again. "Rico, do you still love Chiara?" she asked baldly.

Everything else could be dealt with, but she wasn't about to marry a man in love with another woman.

His upper body tensed and he moved away from her. "My feelings for Chiara are of no concern to you."

"How can you say that?" She shook her head. "You want me to marry you thinking you love another woman. That's cruel, Rico."

"Because *you* love *me,* no?"

Love him? She wanted to brain him. "Don't put words in my mouth. We're talking about your feelings here."

"No. We are not. Anything I felt for Chiara is in the past, as she is."

That sounded somewhat reassuring. If it were the truth.

"Why do you want to marry me?" Perhaps if she

made him face his reasons, he would realize how unrealistic he was being.

"I told you yesterday. I am of an age to marry. Mama, she is expecting a daughter-in-law and I want *bambini*. You and I, we get along, *cara*. We always have. You will make an admirable wife and mother."

That was quite a speech for a man like Rico. "You want to marry me because you think I'll make a good mother?"

He shook his head. "I also believe you will be a good wife. You know my schedule. You know my limitations. You will not expect more than I can give."

Wouldn't she? Perhaps not, but that didn't mean she wouldn't want it. One phrase stuck in her mind though, *she knew his limitations*. He was still hung up on the temporary paralysis. She realized there never had been any real choice. He was vulnerable right now and for a man like Rico that was an anathema. She could not compound that vulnerability by rejecting him.

But she couldn't fool herself into believing her decision was entirely altruistic. If she married Rico, she would once again have a family. She'd been lonely since her mother's death, but never more so than after her father remarried and Pamela had efficiently cut Gianna out of the family circle in everything but name.

The DiRinaldos had been kind, but they had not belonged to her. She had not belonged to them, but if she married Rico that would change. She would once again have a real home, a place in the world she could call her own. And when the babies came, she would have so much more. She could once again share the type of bond she'd shared with her mother.

Only this time she would be the doting mamma.

"I'll marry you."

Andre came back to New York later that night. Gianna was curled up in an armchair watching television in the suite's living room when Andre came in. She knew he'd been to visit Rico and warily waited to see how he would respond to the news she was marrying his brother.

Andre peeled out of his trench coat and hung it over the back of the sofa before sitting down across from her. He measured her with a look. "So, you're going to marry my brother. That's pretty fast work considering he was engaged to Chiara not so long ago."

Gianna felt heat crawl up her neck. "I didn't set out to trap him."

Andre gave her a lazy smile and shrugged. "But you succeeded, *piccola mia*. This is a good thing."

Was it? She'd been plagued with doubts since leaving Rico's room shortly after dinner. She bit her lip, abusing the tender tissue until the pain made her realize what she was doing and she stopped. "He doesn't want to marry me."

"He assured me he did."

"He only thinks that. He's feeling down because he isn't walking yet and Chiara broke off their engagement. As soon as he calms down, he'll regret this craziness."

Andre's smile disappeared. "It is not crazy." He leaned forward, his brown gaze set intently on her. "Rico needs you right now and he recognizes that fact. Hell, I think he has always needed you. He just didn't realize it until he thought he'd lost you for good." So Rico had told Andre about the confrontation with Chiara. "My brother's answer to his need is marriage. Considering how you feel about him, it's the ideal solution."

Men could be so dense. "He won't even tell me if he still loves Chiara."

"He is not that stupid."

"I thought I was pretty smart myself until I agreed to marry Rico." She'd been questioning her intelligence and sanity ever since. What sane woman agreed to marry a man who did not love her, who made no pretense of loving her? Even if that marriage fulfilled the deepest desires of her heart.

Andre shook his head. "But this is a good decision. It is what he wants. It is what you want. What could be better?"

Rico wanting her for the right reasons. She didn't bother saying so. Andre wouldn't get it. In some ways, he and his arrogant brother were too much alike.

"Come. You will have Mama and Papa as your new parents. I as your brother." He pointed at himself with an expansive wave of his hand. "This can only be good."

She was too agitated to respond to his attempt at humor and all too true comment. "You really think I'm doing the right thing?"

Andre reached out and took her hand, squeezing it with his own larger one. "Yes, not only the right thing, but a good thing, *piccola mia*. I will be very pleased to welcome you into our family. And will it not please you to become my sister?"

She nodded, smiling slightly, her worries temporarily assuaged by Andre's wholesale support of her marriage to Rico. But what would his parents think? Would his mother believe Gianna had trapped Rico in a moment of weakness as Andre had jokingly suggested?

The worries kept her awake most of that night and the next two before the wedding.

"Mama will be furious about this register office business." Andre's comment came as he, Rico and Gianna were ushered into the judge's chamber for the short civil ceremony three days after Rico proposed.

Rico turned his head, "She will get over it."

"More likely she'll insist on a church blessing and all the expected conventions of a traditional wedding to accompany it," Andre replied with some humor.

Rico shrugged. "This is fine with me, but she will wait to arrange such a thing until I can walk to the altar."

Rico's insistence on a speedy civil ceremony began to make sense. Gianna had wondered if he had seen their marriage in such a clinical light that he did not want to be bothered by the traditional ceremony. Instead, Rico had not wanted to put himself on display for family and friends in his current condition. Which only drove home the knowledge that his decision to marry her had been made under duress. Andre had told her not to worry about it, but how could she help it?

Rico didn't love her.

As she repeated the short vows, she could not make herself meet Rico's gaze. She kept her eyes lowered, her focus on the small bouquet of white roses Rico had provided. However, when he spoke his vows, he tipped her chin up and said them to her, promising fidelity and honor in a voice that left no doubt to his sincerity. She couldn't help being moved.

The judge gave Rico permission to kiss her and he did, pulling her forward, their heads almost level because he was sitting in the streamlined wheelchair again. The kiss was soft and sweet, leaving her wanting more and yet comforted.

"Congratulazioni, fratello." Andre hugged his brother and kissed Rico's cheeks with typical Italian warmth. Then he turned to Gianna and lifted her off her feet in a bear hug. "Welcome to the family, little sister."

Gianna laughed, despite her misgivings and hugged him back exuberantly. *"Grazie!"*

Andre returned her to her feet and she turned to smile at Rico only to be hit with the unreadability of his expression.

They arrived in Milan in the wee hours of the morning and Gianna sleepily went through customs and then slid into the waiting limo with a tired feeling of relief. She'd slept so little over the past days, it was all she could do to keep her eyes open. Rico and Andre sat on the seat opposite and she knew there was something wrong with that picture.

She was married, but she didn't feel married. It was all so unreal. Rico had pretty much been treating her like a piece of furniture since the wedding. She hadn't expected his undivided attention on the DiRinaldo jet. There'd been several other people present after all. Andre was flying back with them along with the usual complement of security staff and Rico's personal assistant who had been in New York for the past week working with Rico.

Yet, even with the others on board, she hadn't expected him to forget she was even there. He'd spent almost the entire eight-hour flight working. The only time Rico had acknowledged her presence had been at dinner, when the flight attendant, a gorgeous, tall brunette had made a completely unnecessary fuss over Rico.

If Gianna had fussed like that, Rico would have torn strips off her, but he smiled indulgently at the flight attendant. Images of a dinner plate dumped in her new husband's lap had done little to assuage the feeling of jealousy that had plagued her. Which was why Rico was sitting across from her.

She'd waited to get into the limo until he had done so and then sat on the opposite seat. Andre had taken a place beside Rico after only the slightest hesitation.

Focusing her attention out the window, she ignored her new husband's watchful regard and tried to pretend she was alone. It hurt less.

"Papa and Mama will return from their holiday next week." Rico's voice broke the silence.

Gianna said nothing, assuming he'd been speaking to Andre. It wasn't like he'd bothered to speak to her for the last eight hours.

"Gianna."

She didn't turn her gaze from the dark window. "What?"

"You will be happy to see Mama, no?"

"Of course." But was that true? She was still afraid that Rico's parents were going to think she had somehow manipulated Rico while he was vulnerable and wrung a marriage proposal out of him.

"You do not sound enthusiastic."

"I'm tired."

"I do not like speaking to the side of your head, *cara*."

She shifted until their gazes met. It was difficult to read his expression in the limo's dim interior lights. "I got the impression you weren't particularly fond of speaking to me period."

"What is this? When have I ever said such a thing?"

"Actions speak louder than words." The trite saying tripped off her tongue with more venom than she'd meant it to.

He sucked in a breath. "What is your problem?"

Gianna slid her gaze from Rico to Andre to see what he was making of their exchange. The younger man had an inexplicable look of satisfaction on his face. He liked watching his brother argue with his new wife?

"I asked you a question, *cara*."

"And I chose not to answer it." With that, she dismissed him and the irritatingly amused Andre.

In an obvious bid to smooth troubled waters, Andre asked Rico a question and soon the men were making plans for their parents' return. Gianna tuned them out. She was struggling with a horrendous fear that she'd made the biggest mistake of her life. It was obvious Rico was regretting his decision to marry her, but why he couldn't have woken up to reality before the ceremony eluded her.

When they arrived at the DiRinaldo villa, Gianna waited outside the limo for Rico's wheelchair to be unloaded. Rico noticed her waiting and waved her off. "Go inside. There's no reason for you to hover."

Her eyes widened with hurt and she turned on her heel, doing just as he suggested. When she got inside the house, she went directly to the room she always used when she stayed at the villa. There was no way she was going to risk getting kicked out of the master bedroom.

She found a nightgown she'd left behind the summer before and took it into the bathroom. She wrapped her hair turban style in a towel and took a quick shower, washing the feel of extended travel from her skin. Later, she was sitting in front of the vanity mirror, brushing out her hair from the French roll she'd styled it into for her wedding when Rico came in.

"What the hell are you doing *here?*" he demanded.

"Brushing my hair." She flipped her hair over the opposite shoulder and started on the other side. There was absolute silence from where Rico remained near the door.

When she had removed every tangle from her hair, she parted it into three sections and started braiding it for sleep.

"Don't."

The harsh demand startled her and her fingers stilled in their task. She heard the wheelchair moving across the floor, but she couldn't make herself face him.

"*Per l'amore di cielo,* it is beautiful." His fingers threaded through the tresses, undoing the beginnings of the braid. "I have wanted to see it like this, but it is more than I could imagine."

She peeked a look at him through the curtain of her hair and her breath caught at the look of intense concentration on his face. "You like my hair?"

It seemed like such an inconsequential thing. She wore it long because her mother had liked it that way and letting it grow had been a way to feel close to her. It would never have occurred to her that Rico might find her very ordinary locks so fascinating, but he did.

His attention was riveted.

"Come here." He went to pull her into his lap, but self-preservation had her shooting to her feet and moving away.

"I'm tired. I want to go to bed."

Rico's eyes glittered silver messages at her she did not want to read. "I too wish to go to bed."

"Then you'd better get to it, hadn't you?"

He drew himself into a stiff and imposing stance. Even in the wheelchair, he was easily as tall as her and a hundred times more intimidating. "You plan that I should return to my bed, while you sleep here?"

She shrugged, trying for an insouciance she did not feel. "What difference does it make?" She'd meant that since he did not love her or particularly want her, he shouldn't care where she slept.

His head reared back as if she'd slapped him. "Indeed, what difference, *cara*? I cannot perform the usual wedding night ritual and undoubtedly the thought of sharing my bed is not a welcome one."

"That's not what I—"

"It does not matter," he said, cutting across her words. "It is just as well to me if you do not expect me to perform my husbandly duties. They hold little appeal when I cannot participate fully and are unnecessary to the conception of our child.''

The words were like icy rain stinging her with their frozen cruelty. She stood there in mute pain while he spun his chair and left her room.

She walked to the bed, feeling like an old woman, all the energy necessary to braid her hair drained by Rico's cold rejection. He saw the most beautiful experience of her life as a duty…an unnecessary one at that. And unappealing. How he must have despised her wanton eagerness to experience pleasure at his hands while incapable of giving any back.

Even if Rico had not been paralyzed, she would not have known how to return his caresses. Chiara had been right. Gianna was not enough woman for a man like Rico, regardless of his condition. Why had he wanted to marry her, then?

The answer came in another blinding wave of pain. Because he didn't love her or want her. She could give him babies, but she would not be a constant reminder of what he could not have. She didn't know what would happen when Rico regained feeling in the lower half of his body. Regret for their marriage would play a major role in his feelings, she was sure of it.

CHAPTER SIX

RICO sat on the balcony above the swimming pool and watched Andre and Gianna cavort in the water. It was a scene like so many he had witnessed in the past. Gianna and Andre had always played together, being of almost the same age. But now she was his wife and Rico was seeing his brother as a rival male rather than her childhood playmate.

The feelings of jealousy surging through him were unwelcome. He had not expected them to be part of marriage, but then he had not expected to sleep alone in the marital bed either. Even so, he didn't want to feel jealous of his own brother and the woman he had married. He simply had not anticipated experiencing such an emotion toward Gianna. He'd never been particularly jealous of Chiara. Possessive, yes, but jealous, no.

It made no sense. It was not as if he was in love with his wife. He cared for her. Of course he did. She had been a part of the fabric of his life since her birth.

Their mothers had been best friends as children and behaved as sisters as adults. Gianna's mother, Eliana, had married an American professor and returned to the States with him, while his mother had moved to Milan after marrying his father. But the two women's families had shared holidays and visits until Gianna's mother died. Gianna had continued to come to stay with his family, more frequently after her father remarried.

She did not play emotional games like Chiara. Chiara had used sex to manipulate and even before the accident, Rico had been growing increasingly intolerant of her tactics for getting what she wanted. He had believed marriage to Gianna would have all the benefits of the wedded state without making him vulnerable again to a woman. Gianna was too innocent and too good to manipulate him as his former fiancée had done.

Even so, he'd been wrong.

He'd felt damn vulnerable when she rejected him sexually the night before. He'd been sure that in this area he could at least give her the semblance of a normal marriage. She'd gone to pieces in his arms when he touched her in the hotel suite, letting him make love to her with a sweet trust he'd found addictive.

He'd suspected she had tender feelings for him before that. She had made it to his bedside after the accident before his brother. And according to a scornful Chiara and equally admiring Andre, Gianna had not left Rico's side until he came out of coma. Awareness of her devotion had buoyed him when so much had seemed hopeless.

After making love to her, he had been sure she had stronger feelings than friendship toward him. No woman responded with such speed and abandon without feeling something powerful for the man making love to her.

So, why the hell had she rejected him last night?

They hadn't spent much time together on the plane. He'd had to work. At least making money was something he could do unhindered without the use of his legs. At dinner, she hadn't seemed to care when the flight attendant flirted with him, and for some reason that had irritated him. So, even though he'd found the other woman's cloying attentions annoying, he had suffered them in some ridiculous attempt to get a rise out of Gianna.

It hadn't worked and he'd ended up feeling angry and stupid. Hadn't he told Gianna that he did not play those kind of games? He had enjoyed feeling like an idiot even less than his present jealousy. So, he'd been short with her in the limousine and felt guilty for being that way. But she'd got her own back. She had ignored him.

He still had not expected to find her occupying a guest room instead of his bedroom when he made it up the stairs. He'd gone to her room breathing fire to be poleaxed by the sight of that gorgeous hair streaming down her body. It had rippled like living silk and he had wanted to touch it with a hunger he had not been willing to analyze.

He'd done so. And it had only made him want more. More of her soft skin. More of her. But when he'd gone to pull her to him, she had backed away. She'd lost no time making it clear she had no interest in sharing his bed.

The rejection still stung and watching his brother play with her in a way he could not, was doing nothing to improve Rico's temper.

Gianna approached the room set aside for Rico's physical therapy with some trepidation. She'd avoided him the entire morning, shared stilted conversation with him and Andre over lunch and had only ventured down here in order to meet the new physical therapist. It was silly, but she needed to assure herself that Rico was truly in good hands. Besides, she'd been participating in Rico's therapy since the beginning.

She stepped into the room that looked so much like the one used for the same purpose at the hospital and stopped to marvel at how quickly the transformation had taken place. The warm wood décor had been replaced with exercise mats, a set of parallel bars, a treatment table and assorted weight lifting equipment. The big windows still allowed the sun to stream in through the clear glass, which was a great improvement over the hospital's fluorescent lighting.

Rico lay on the treatment table. A man with steel-gray hair and a very fit body encased in white cotton trousers and T-shirt put Rico's legs through the usual stretching exercises. Rico's own clothes resembled those he'd worn for sessions in New York and had the same destabilizing effect on her nervous system. She had to concentrate on getting her breath to come more naturally before she greeted the two men.

"Good afternoon."

Rico's head swiveled toward her, an expression she could not decipher in his eyes. *"Buon giorno."*

The therapist turned around. "Hello. You must be Mrs. DiRinaldo. I am Timothy Stephens. Rico tells me you are newlyweds. Congratulations."

"Thank you, Dr. Stephens. I didn't realize you would be English," she blurted out.

"Canadian, actually, and please call me Tim. A colleague of mine in New York recommended me to your husband."

She felt foolish for not distinguishing the accents.

Her only excuse was the shock she'd experienced that the therapist wasn't Italian. "I hope your temporary relocation wasn't a problem for you."

Tim laughed. It was a warm, rich sound, reminding her of her father's laughter when her mother had been alive. "My wife would have killed me if I had turned down an opportunity to work in Milan, all expenses paid. She's out shoe shopping as we speak."

Gianna felt her mouth crease upward in response to the man's friendly manner. "You'll have to bring her to the villa for dinner after Rico's parents return from their trip. I'm sure they'll want to meet her."

"Thank you. I will."

The whole time they'd been talking, Tim had not hesitated in his ministrations on Rico's legs. He now laid the one he had been exercising on the table and began an examination, testing for feeling. Not only did Rico confirm feeling in his toes and feet, but he actually moved his right foot in the beginnings of a rotating movement.

Gianna rushed to his side and grabbed his arm. "You didn't tell me you'd regained some movement."

"It is hardly more than a twitch, *cara*. Nothing to get so excited about."

She stared at him, unable to believe his cool demeanor. "You've got to be kidding! I was ecstatic when you felt your toes…that twitch you're so nonchalant about is cause for major celebration."

"Is it really, *tesoro?*"

And suddenly memories of what had happened when she had *celebrated* his first milestone filled her mind. She'd leapt on him and they'd kissed. Her gaze skittered to his lips. They were curled in a sardonic smile, but all she could think about was matching her mouth to his.

"I think all celebrations of the sort you are contemplating will have to wait, no?"

His mocking tone brought her back to the present with a bump. He didn't want her. He found kissing her a duty, a chore, not his preferred method of celebration.

She turned her heated face away from the men and pretended an interest in the parallel bars at the other end of the room. She was embarrassed by his comment as well as hurt remembering how little she fulfilled his needs as a woman.

"How soon do you think before Rico will be using these?" she asked Tim regarding the parallel bars.

"That's difficult to gauge. Every patient has their own timeline of healing, but your husband has a strong will and with a new wife, a pretty good incentive to recover as quickly as possible. We could see him using those in as little as seven days."

She spun around at such good news, only to be stopped short by Rico's cold voice. "I am a man, no? I do not need to be spoken of as a child who has no say in his future."

His masculine ego was definitely out of kilter.

Gianna wasn't sure how to assuage Rico's anger, but Tim just smiled.

"It's a bad habit family members and doctors can fall into. Talking about a patient as if he's not there. Thanks for calling us on it. How do you feel about targeting a goal of seven days for preliminary work on the bars?''

''It is doable,'' Rico replied with a confidence that pleased Gianna.

That confidence seemed well placed as he steadily regained feeling up his legs. Rico pushed himself mercilessly, doing more therapy sessions than he had in the hospital. Gianna still attended the sessions with him, but he seemed to need her encouragement less and less.

It was as if something inside him had clicked and even the DiRinaldo bank and Enterprises took back-seat to his drive to walk again.

''Still, there is no feeling from the knees up,'' he said to Tim a few days later. ''How can I use the bars with only half my legs working?''

Tim smiled as he helped Rico move from the weight lifting machine back to his chair. ''You're doing great. You'll be on the bars in no time.''

''It has been six days. Tomorrow is seven.''

''You're almost there,'' Tim said with an insouciance Gianna envied as he packed up his supplies.

She wished she could respond in such a relaxed fashion to Rico, but she couldn't.

Tim promised to be in early the next morning for a session.

''It is easy for him to dismiss this. He does not sit useless in a wheelchair.'' Rico's frustration didn't surprise her, but his voicing it did. He'd been stoic about everything since returning to Italy. And very distant.

She handed him a small towel to wipe the sweat from his brow. He'd been working on his upper body tone and his muscles rippled with the effects of weight training.

"Only a fool would call you useless, Rico."

"But what else can I be? My wife, she sleeps in a separate bed. My business, it must run itself while I retrain my body to function normally. Do not spout these happy platitudes at me."

She felt herself blushing. They'd never discussed their wedding night. She assumed he was glad she stayed in the other room considering his attitude toward making love to her.

"If your business is running itself then why do you spend so much time on the computer and phone, not to mention attending board meetings at the bank?" He'd gone to one yesterday, intent on proving to the other stockholders that all was well.

According to Andre, Rico had been very convincing.

She wasn't surprised.

"I notice you ignore the reality of separate beds."

The blush intensified and she turned away, wanting to hide her vulnerability to him. "We both know why I don't sleep with you, Rico. It's not as if our marriage is real."

Strong fingers curled around her wrist and pulled until she faced him. "And why is our marriage not real?" The molten metal of his gaze burned into her. "You agreed to have my baby, to be my wife. I made vows to you. What is not real about this?"

"Y-you weren't thinking straight. Now that you've had some time to think about it, I'm sure you've come to your senses." She tried to smile as if the words she was saying weren't tearing her into a million pieces. "We can get an annulment. No one need ever know about our crazy wedding."

He tugged her a step closer, his body exuding dangerous energy. "Andre knows. I know. You vowed to be my wife."

"But you didn't really want to marry me. You know you didn't. I knew you'd come to your senses and you have."

"On what do you draw this conclusion?"

What could she say? *You find kissing me a chore.* That would sound like she cared, which she did, but she didn't want him to know that. She had very little pride left where he was concerned, but she didn't want what remained lacerated.

When she didn't answer immediately, his eyes narrowed. "Perhaps it is not that you believe I have changed my mind, but that you have changed yours."

She shook her head. "No. I feel the same way I did when I agreed to marry you," she answered honestly.

He held her gaze captive with his own, his eyes drilling into her with ruthless determination. What was he looking for?

For her part, she was becoming increasingly aware of his physical person. His scent tantalized her, made her think of things she'd tried desperately to forget since leaving New York. He smelled earthy, his sweat-covered skin irresistibly drawing her gaze and to look was to want. To want was to remember and to remember was madness. Yet, she could not turn off the images in her mind.

"You pity me?" he asked, shocking her.

"What?"

"You pitied me. You did not wish to marry me, but you felt too sorry for me to reject me. You hoped I would let you go, but I have not done this."

She stared at him, completely aghast. "Pity?" she squeaked. Who could pity Rico? He was too vital, too much a man. "You've got the wrong end of the stick."

He glared at her and she felt guilty even though she knew she wasn't guilty of what he'd accused her of. "Is it also this wrong end of the stick for me to believe my parents will share in your pity when they realize my wife will not share my bed?"

"I didn't refuse to share your bed," she practically shouted.

"Then you will not be bothered to learn I have instructed the maid to move your things to my suite."

He'd done what? "But, Rico—"

"If you married me out of pity, I ask you allow that emotion to prompt you to sleeping in my bed. It is not as if I am a risk to your virtue."

"I don't pity you!"

"But you also do not wish to be married to me."

"I didn't say that."

"Then what is this talk of annulments?"

"I thought you wanted out."

"I did not say this. I do not want this," he said with emphasis. "Marriage is for a lifetime."

She groaned. "I knew you thought that."

"I do not think it; I know it."

"But, you don't *have* to stay married to me."

"Enough of this." He threw her hand from him in violent repudiation. "You want out of our marriage. You say so. Do not hide behind a false concern for *my* wants. You are my wife because I chose you for my wife. You cannot really believe I want to end our marriage before it has even begun."

The hot sulfur of his glare singed her tender emotions. "You do not want to be the mother of my *bambini*. Fine. *Non è un problema.* Go." He waved his hand toward the door. "But go before my parents come tomorrow. I will have enough sympathy to deal with without explaining a wife who is no wife."

Pain coursed through her so she could barely breathe. For the second time, she was being told to leave Rico's life. Only this time by him. If she went, would he ever let her back in?

Apparently, he truly did want to remain married. Knowing that, could she leave him? *Did she want to leave him?* The answer was simply no.

"I don't want out of our marriage." She whispered the words because she couldn't speak more loudly past the obstruction in her throat.

"Then you sleep in my bed."

She nodded and turned to go, her heart aching from a choice that had been no choice at all. Share a bed with a man who saw touching her as an unpleasant duty or be evicted forever from the life of the man she loved.

Crunch time came that night when she walked into Rico's suite to find him getting ready for bed.

The cool blue tones and Mediterranean-style wood furniture hardly registered on her consciousness.

He was sitting on the edge of the huge bed, half dressed. He'd taken off the immaculate suit he'd worn at dinner. His tie was gone and his shirt hung open on his torso. Short black hair curled across his chest and down to the navy-blue silk boxers that rode low on his hips.

He was just so gorgeous, it was criminal. No one man should be allowed to have so much sex appeal.

How was she going to sleep tonight with all that male perfection lying within inches of her body? Okay, on the oversize king bed, maybe it would be feet, but she didn't think the width of the room would be enough. What if he slept naked? She didn't think she could handle it. She was already on sensory overload and he still had his shirt and boxers on.

She gulped and met his eyes, her breathing already erratic.

He was looking at her with an arrested expression.

Maybe he'd never seen a woman do an imitation of a blushing, gasping fish before. Must be entertaining from his perspective.

"I... Where's my nightgown?" she asked, for lack of anything better to say.

"Do you need it?" he asked, with a positively wicked gleam in his eyes.

"Do I need it?" she repeated, her mind finding it impossible to wrap around the concept of going to bed naked.

"Many husbands and wives sleep together without wearing anything, no?"

Was that humor in his voice? She could hardly credit it, not after his mood earlier. "Are you going to sleep that way?"

"What way?"

He was tormenting her and loving it.

She took a deep breath and let it out. "Without your shorts." She was proud of the ability to get the words out when her mind had gone on an erotic vacation.

"I do not like confinement in my sleep."

"Oh… I think I prefer wearing a nightgown."

He shrugged as if it did not matter one way or the other to him. Which she was sure it didn't. He wasn't the one practically hyperventilating at the thought of sleeping together in the same bed.

"Uh—where is it?"

"In there." He indicated the walk-in closet on the other side of the room.

She almost tripped over her feet in her haste to get to the relative privacy of the closet. She found her nightgowns hanging at one end of the wardrobe. She chose a white one with an embroidered yoke and no sleeves. It was unseasonably warm for late September in Milan.

She took her time in the bathroom, hoping Rico would already be under the covers when she returned to the bedroom.

She got her wish, for all the good it did her. He sat, propped up against pillows, his upper body naked and the bedclothes hitting him low enough to be indecent. She stopped and stared at the sight he presented for several seconds.

"Are you coming to bed, *cara?*"

She swallowed and nodded, speech beyond her.

It took all her strength of will to cross that room and climb into the opposite side of the bed from him. What would she do if she snuggled up to him in the night? What if she had one of the sensual dreams that had plagued her since the night in New York? The dreams in which he played center stage. And what if her body acted out the fantasy with him so close? She'd woken up wrapped around a pillow on more than one occasion, her lower body throbbing.

She lay beneath the covers, stiff with nerves.

"You look like a thirteenth-century bride waiting to be ravished by her despot husband."

Her head whipped sideways to see gleaming silver eyes and a sardonically twisted mouth on his handsome face.

"I'm not used to sleeping with anyone."

"We established that in New York."

She nodded.

"I thought we also established you liked my touch, no?"

She thought about denying it. Her pride begged her to, but innate honesty wouldn't let her. "Yes."

"Yet you have refused to share my bed since our wedding night."

"You said it was a duty. You didn't like it." Tears pricked her eyes with pained remembrance.

His look sliced into her. "A man may say many things after his woman rejects him, no?"

"I didn't reject you." How could he believe that? She wanted him. Desperately. It had to be obvious.

"You did."

Remembering how she'd pulled away, she bit her lip. "Maybe a little, but I didn't mean it the way you took it."

"And how should I have taken it?"

"Not as a big rejection," she answered rather lamely and then added, "I was jealous and angry," with more honesty.

"Of what were you jealous?"

"You seemed to ignore me on the flight and then you let the flight attendant fawn over you, but when we got here, you took me to task for just waiting outside the limousine for you."

He sighed, his expression pained. "I thought you

did not notice. I thought you did not care. So, I tolerated her annoying behavior to try to make you care. I felt really stupid afterward and that made me lash out at you.''

Was he telling her the truth? He hadn't tried to make Chiara jealous, but he'd admitted to wanting to make Gianna jealous. That was a major admission for a man like Rico. ''It wasn't meant as a big rejection,'' she repeated, with more conviction this time.

''For a man, any sexual rejection is big, *cara mia*. Did you not know this?''

''No.'' She sighed. It was hard to believe he had not realized how very much she wanted him, but as impossible as it seemed to her, she had hurt him. ''I'm sorry.''

''Are you really, *tesoro?*''

Her heart just melted every time he called her that. It was so much more intimate than *cara*. An endearment reserved for her alone...or that is how she felt. She'd never heard him use it with Chiara, or anyone else.

''Yes,'' she replied, a little breathless. Who wouldn't be, two tiny feet from a man as sexy as Rico?

''Show me.''

CHAPTER SEVEN

GIANNA didn't move, unable to believe what Rico had just said. Show him? How?

He reached across the width dividing them and tugged on her wrist. *"Venuto a me."*

His huskily growled command to come to him sparked an instant ache deep in her core while his grip on her wrist kindled an uncontrollable desire for more of his touch. She stared at him, feeling like a small animal mesmerized by a predator ready to pounce.

Did he mean what she thought he meant?

"W-why?" she managed to stutter out in a whisper past a throat as dry as the sand in the Sahara.

The tug on her wrist increased. "Come here and you will find out."

How could seven little words short-circuit her brain and send her pulses rioting? She loved him. She wanted him. She'd been pining for his touch since New York. She felt more alive right now with just his fingers circling her wrist than she had any time in the week since their wedding.

That knowledge along with a trick of the light that made him look vulnerable undermined any resistance she might have considered putting up. At least that is what she told herself as she docilely allowed him to pull her to his side. Once there, she lay in total silence, wondering what came next.

"Sit up."

Captivated by the intense sensuality that seemed to come off him like an electric force field, she did as he said without a murmur. She knelt beside him, her knees centimeters from his powerful thigh. She could now see he'd left on the silk boxers. In deference to her feelings?

"Unbraid your hair, *tesoro*."

She didn't know why, but she felt compelled to obey the enthrallingly sexy voice of her husband. She carefully undid her braid, finger-combing the long chestnut strands into a curtain down her back and over one shoulder. He watched her with deep concentration that made her hands tremble.

When she was done, he reached out and ran his fingers through the hair covering her shoulder and breast. "So soft."

She shivered as the pads of his fingers brushed over her nipple in their path to the end of her hair. He smiled and repeated the entire process, beginning his long caress in the hair at her nape and following it down again, but this time when he reached her breast, he stopped. He cupped her and rubbed her nipple into more pronounced arousal. The sensation of hair brushing against the thin fabric of her nightgown over her very sensitive flesh sent her nerve endings into orbit.

"Take off your nightgown," he commanded gutturally.

Her breath caught somewhere between her breastbone and expelling. She didn't think she could do it. She wasn't one of his experienced lovers, used to undressing for a man. Gianna had never been nude with any man but Rico. She shook her head.

"Do you want me to stop touching you?"

How could he ask such a stupid question? He'd barely begun and she felt as if her entire body had gone on red alert. "No."

"Then take off your gown." The sensual threat in his voice enervated her, but he merely dropped his hand to his side and watched her. Waiting.

"You're being bossy again," she whispered.

He shrugged.

That's all. Just a shrug. No words. No other movement. He was leaving it completely up to her. She could either remove her gown or...or what? Turn over and go to sleep? She almost laughed at the ludicrousness of that thought. Her sane mind demanded she give it credence, but her body throbbed for what it knew Rico could give...pleasure beyond comprehension.

Did it really matter if he saw this as some kind of duty when he did it so well?

When he touched her, she felt loved. She knew she wasn't, but she would face that truth afterward— for now the heated potential of fulfilled passion lured her like a siren's song. If she ended up crashed and broken on the rocks of unrequited love, at least the journey there would have been more satisfying than the endless ocean of loneliness she'd known for so long.

Her decision made, she began pulling her gown up her body and over her head. Warm, sure hands cupped the undersides of her breasts when the fabric was still blocking her head. The sensation was so incredible, her entire body stopped movement in arrested delight. Which left her literally in the dark.

Rico abraded her nipples with his thumbs. Drawing concentric circles around them until she thought she would go mad with desire. She groaned and arched into his touch, her entire being focused on those two small peaks and the pleasure they were receiving.

He gave a growling laugh and one hand abandoned her breast. She made a sound of protest and then felt her nightgown being pulled the rest of the way off. Suddenly she could see him as well as feel him. And what a sight it was. His eyes were lambent with desire, his chest rippled as he moved to pull her into the circle of his arms. She landed against the short curling hair of his chest and shuddered in reaction to the feel of her body against his without the barrier of clothing, except those barely there silk boxers, for the first time.

"*Si*, yes, it feels right, no?"

She kissed the hollow between his neck and shoulder, lingering to taste the salty goodness of his skin and inhale the spicy scent that was distinctly Rico. "Yes."

The arm around her waist tightened and she squeaked, finding it difficult to breathe. He loosened his hold immediately, but she was so proud of the reaction she'd caused she repeated the kiss, this time licking his skin delicately along his collarbone. He molded her breast, pinching her nipple and sending arcs of sensation to her most feminine place.

Then his other hand moved until he was cupping her backside, his fingers flirting with the vulnerable softness at the apex of her thighs. She squirmed against his touch, seeking remembered pleasure with blind passion. He flipped her onto her back and loomed above her, his body angled and resting on one elbow. "I want to make love to you."

"Yes."

The word was barely out of her mouth when his lips were over hers. She gasped in a mixture of shock and bliss. He immediately deepened the kiss, taking command of her mouth in a way that left her breathless and aching for more. While he kissed her with a fervor she found completely overwhelming, his free hand brushed up and down her body in repeated erotic caresses that left her shivering and craving a more intimate touch.

He broke the kiss and her starving lungs sucked in air.

"You are so responsive, *piccola mia*."

She'd never felt less like a child, but she wasn't sure her all out abandoned response was a good thing. Maybe he liked a more composed partner. Judging by Chiara, Gianna knew he was used to a more sophisticated one. "I can't help it," she admitted, not without a little embarrassment.

His look was pure, primitive male. "I don't want you to."

"Oh."

She bit her lip, wondering why he'd stopped kissing her, why his hand was motionless against her waist.

Then he did something she found very odd. He carefully arranged her hair over the pillow, taking so much time she was throbbing for more of his touch when he was finished.

"Why did you do that?"

"I have dreamed of seeing you like this."

Could that be true? "You dreamed of me?" She couldn't accept that a man who saw touching her as some kind of chore would dream about it.

He didn't answer. Instead, he picked up a lock of her hair and using it like a paint brush, began to "paint" her body, paying particular attention to her breasts and nipples. He was so focused in his efforts, she felt unsettled by his attention. He didn't seem to notice that her body was a little too curvy by today's fashion standards. If the look on his face was any indication, it didn't bother him a bit that she was easily six inches shorter than Chiara and both a bra and dress size bigger.

The length of her hair allowed him to tease her bellybutton and he did so, in such an erotic way she was soon moving shamelessly in a mindless search for relief from the torment pulsing between her legs.

She wanted to touch him and reached out to do so, but he stopped her. "No."

"Why?"

"This is for you, *tesoro.*"

"I want it to be for you too," she replied.

He ignored her words, kissing her into total submission. Speaking in Italian, he told her how sexy she was, how beautiful he found her body and its assorted bits. Some of his words were so frank, they embarrassed her, but she found them all arousing.

Why wouldn't he touch her where she needed to be touched?

She realized she'd made the demand out loud when he laughed. "In time, *tesoro.* Making love to a virgin should not be rushed, no?"

"This virgin wouldn't mind," she assured him.

But he just laughed again and continued with the maddening caresses. She cried out in relief when his mouth closed over one nipple. But her relief soon turned to wanton need that remained unfulfilled. He suckled her until she was crying with desire. She begged him to stop. He moved to the other breast. By the time he was done with that one, she was a shaking, gasping bundle of over sensitized flesh.

His hand moved to the soft curls between her legs and teased her with light touches. "You belong to me."

"Yes." How could he doubt it?

His finger dipped between her legs, finding the evidence of her excitement. She widened her legs, no longer caring if her actions betrayed her overpowering need for him. He caressed her like he had the last time, gently circling her bud of feminine pleasure and then rubbing it in alternative movements until she came with an ecstatic scream that reverberated in her eardrums long after it was over.

His hand stilled, but he did not take it away. She lay, inert, wondering if he would do as he had in New York and touch her into senselessness.

He kissed her. Softly. Possessively.

His hand moved and she felt flesh inside her body for the first time as he probed her opening with the tip of his finger. The sensation was incredible.

"That feels good," she blurted out.

He smiled, elemental male claiming his woman. "It will feel better," he promised and his finger dipped in further.

Incredibly, her body responded with renewed ardor and she could feel the build of yet another explosion in her innermost places. He probed further and suddenly she felt pain. She tried to back away from it, but he wouldn't let her move.

"Trust me."

She met his silver gaze and stopped trying to get

away. She nodded as tears stung her eyes from the discomfort.

His thumb teased her sweet spot while he pushed inexorably forward into her until the burning became almost unbearable. His mouth closed over her left nipple as he pushed through the barrier and pressed into her body in an intimate way she would not have believed possible in their current circumstance.

Then pain turned to unutterable pleasure as he made love to her with the moves of a man who knew exactly what he was doing.

Pleasure built and built and built until her entire body was shaking on the edge of going over. He gently bit her nipple and everything inside her convulsed in the most incredible wave of ecstasy she could ever have imagined.

Fireworks were too tame to describe it.

A supernova too distant to express the intimacy of it.

Love was the only word that could possibly describe her body's reaction to her husband's lovemaking.

She shuddered every time he moved his hand, experiencing aftershocks course through her time and again until she fell into a dozing stupor.

She felt him move beside her and then the depression of the bed as he lifted himself off and onto his chair. She couldn't get her glued eyelids open enough to see what he was doing.

Time went by. She didn't know how long, but at some point he returned to their bed. She felt a warm washcloth between her legs. She twitched, made self-conscious by his actions, but he gentled her with a caress. "Shh, *tesoro*. Let me do this. It is a husband's honorable right."

Still reeling from the other "honorable right" he had exercised, she relaxed and let him complete his ministrations, feeling cherished if a little embarrassed.

Afterward he pulled her to his side, his solid, muscular arm closing around her with the warmth of a security blanket. "This, what I do with you. It is not a duty."

Remembering his words of praise, his passion filled kisses, she believed him. They'd both lashed out and said things they hadn't meant, but he liked touching her. He'd made that very, very clear. She smiled, sleepily, content. She snuggled into him and mouthed words of love against his skin before settling against his body.

On the verge of unconsciousness she heard him say, "There can be no annulment now."

She wanted to ask him what he meant, but she was too tired.

Gianna swam to wakefulness with a sense of disorientation. Why was her bed so warm? She couldn't move her head. Panic at the thought lessened only fractionally as she registered the fact her hair was trapped under something preventing her movement. A heavy weight was settled across her ribs as well. An arm. An arm whose hand was positioned possessively over one of her breasts. *Rico*.

Oh, Mother. Her eyes flew open to warm Italian sunshine and the supine form of the man beside her. Neither of them was wearing a stitch of clothes. The sheet covered the lower half of his body, but both their upper bodies were cast in stark relief by the bright morning light. His dark hand over the pale skin of her breast sent a shiver of alarm through her.

What had she done?

She'd let Rico make love to her. That's what. A very personal ache between her legs attested to it.

She hadn't known a man could do what he had done to her with his hand. Thinking of how intimately he had touched her brought a rush of embarrassed heat up her skin and her gaze was drawn irresistibly back to his sleeping form.

His face was relaxed in sleep, appearing younger, not so intimidating; but not even unconsciousness could dispel the arrogant set of his mouth. His dark hair was mussed and stubble shadowed his jaw. Seeing him like this felt infinitely special, as private as what they had shared the night before.

But they hadn't shared it, her mind taunted her. He'd refused to let her touch him. Why? Unable to resist the urge, she reached up and very softly brushed back a lock of black hair falling rakishly over his forehead. After his insistence she keep her hands to herself the night before, she felt like a cat burglar, sneaking in to steal the family silver.

Emboldened when he did not wake up, she allowed her fingers to trail over his hair-roughened chest as she had longed to do before. It felt strange. The hair was both soft and springy, different from her own body hair which was much finer and of course nowhere near as prevalent. She tentatively pressed her finger into his flesh and reveled in the hard strength of his muscles. He was just so beautiful. A secret smile tipped the corner of her lips.

It would mortally offend Rico to be described as

beautiful, she knew. But to her, he was everything masculine beauty could be. Strong. Virile. Hard. And big. He was so much bigger than her. Lying beside him emphasized the difference in their sizes. It made her feel safe. He stirred and she snatched her hand back, her heart palpitating at a terrifying rate at the thought of getting caught both ogling and touching him like a small child with a new toy.

He didn't move again and she let out a rush of air from tight lungs. Would he be bothered to waken to her touch? She wished she knew more about men and what made them tick. Rico was the only man she'd ever been interested in and he was as incomprehensible to her as a Chinese word puzzle.

But he'd shared a little of himself last night. He'd admitted to wanting to make her jealous. He'd also told her that touching her was not a duty. It was a fair start.

And he had been emphatic that he wanted their marriage to continue. Comprehension of the meaning of his final words hit her with the force of a Tae Kwon Do ax kick. Rico had "consummated" their marriage last night. She was no longer a virgin and that ruled out an annulment. He'd done it on purpose. Of course he had, but she couldn't be angry about that. Not when his actions were further proof of just how permanently he wanted them to stay together.

She smiled at the thought even as Rico's arm shifted, telling her he was waking for real this time.

He opened his eyes and silver light caught her gaze as inexorably as a high-powered magnet trapping a paper clip.

"*Buona mattina.*" His voice was husky from sleep.

She was now very aware of his hand against her breast. "Good morning," she croaked with something less than sophisticated cool.

"Is it?" His eyes probed hers.

He needed her reassurance. She didn't mind giving it to him. "Yes." Feeling embarrassed by their new intimacy, she tried to move away, but his arms gave no quarter. "We need to get up. You have a session in less than an hour." Now that he was awake, she realized she wanted to avoid a postmortem on the night before.

He might want to stay married to her, but he didn't love her and that colored the night before gray around the edges.

"What is wrong, *cara?* Are you sore?" he asked, with what she considered an extreme lack of tact.

She averted her gaze. How did other women deal with this first morning after? "A little."

His hand tipped her chin until she was forced to look into his eyes. "I regret I had to hurt you."

She could read the sincerity in his expression. She didn't want him to feel guilty for something so natural. "No big deal." She tried to sound as sophisticated as she wished she felt. "It's usually at least a little painful the first time, I've always heard."

"Less painful maybe than if it had been a normal first time, no? You are very tight, little one."

This was going too far. "Rico! I don't think we need to discuss the particulars."

His smile sent her thoughts exploding in different directions, none of them rational. "It is nothing for which you should feel shy with me, *tesoro.* I am your husband."

Remembering a similar statement he had made after goading her into admitting her virginity, she said, "Rico, your idea of what should and should not embarrass me is nowhere near my own."

"You are very innocent."

"Not anymore," she was provoked into saying.

He looked so smug. "No, *tesoro*. Not any longer. Now, you belong to me."

"For better or worse." A tinge of unexpected bitterness laced her voice. What was wrong with her?

He frowned. "You are not happy to be married to me? I do not believe this after last night."

Could a guy get any more conceited?

"Face it, Rico. This marriage is not what either of us envisioned for our future." And it was only as she said the words, she realized how true they were. Rico had planned to marry supermodel beauty and she, well she had planned to marry for love.

He brushed her cheek in an oddly tender gesture. "This is true, but life is rarely what we expect, no?"

"I guess you're right." She let her hand rest against his chest, over his heart. The steady beat was reassuring. "I always expected to marry because of love."

His arm tightened around her and an expression she could not identify hardened his features. "You love me."

She opened her mouth, to say what she didn't know.

He forestalled her. "Do not deny the gift of your heart to me." He put his finger over her lips, sealing them shut. "I will treasure it always."

Rather than confirm or deny his words, she voiced her own worry. "You don't love me."

What had been a difficult expression to interpret

became no expression at all. "I care for you, *tesoro*. I will be faithful." Again that soft brush of fingers along her temple and cheek. "We will have a good life."

She didn't answer. She couldn't. Knowing something and hearing it were two very different animals she discovered at that moment. She'd known Rico didn't love her, but secretly she'd nursed a hope that his insistence on marriage and keeping their marriage had meant something more than it did. Hearing him say he only cared for her and they would have a good life was like taking a mortal blow and yet having her opponent expect her to remain standing.

Rico wasn't her enemy, but at that moment he hurt her more than all her stepmother's petty cruelties over the years had been capable of doing. Years of loneliness in her marriage, longing for a love he did not feel stretched out before Gianna. But, perhaps the most lowering thought of all was that those years looked infinitely more devastating without Rico in them.

She took a deep breath and let it out, concentrating on not allowing her devastated emotions to show in her voice. "We still need to get up."

He looked like he was going to pursue the discussion further. She could not stand it.

"Please," she begged, not caring if she sounded pathetic at that point. She could not bear one more minute of their current conversation.

He wasn't feeling merciful because he shook his head. "I cannot let you go looking as you do. You must trust me that our marriage will be all that a marriage should be."

"Did you love Chiara?" she asked with masochistic fervor.

"With Chiara, it was sex. I thought there was more at the time, but I find now my memories of our time together center on one activity."

She didn't like the thought of him remembering sex with Chiara. Complete sex. Something they could not yet experience. "And with me?" she asked.

"It is infinitely more."

"But not love," she said, wondering why she was putting herself through this.

His mouth hardened while his mind searched for words. When they came, they were not what she needed to hear. "We have a history."

"You and Chiara have a history, too."

"Chiara is the past. You are the present."

"The wife you don't love, but refuse to let go."

"And do you wish to go?"

She swallowed, incapable of uttering a face-saving lie.

He pulled her across his chest, exciting her flesh even as she tried to come to terms with her emotions. He stopped when her face was directly above his, her lips only centimeters from his own. "I know you do not."

"You're right." Leaving him would be like severing a limb from her body without anesthetic. But living without his love would be as painful as constantly chafing an open wound.

"I do not wish you to go either."

Looking into eyes that demanded she believe his words, she felt a small spark of hope ignite. He did not want to let her go. That had to mean something.

Maybe he did not love her, but they had a lifetime together. Surely he would eventually figure out she was the best woman in the world for him. After all, Rico was smart.

He gave up on words at that point and kissed her.

The kiss turned carnal in less than five seconds and soon his hands were roaming over the naked contours of her back and exposed bottom with possessive assurance.

She fell into the lovemaking without protest, needing the physical intimacy more than ever after the denial of emotional ties.

They were late for Rico's physical therapy, but Tim only laughed, ribbing them about being newlyweds. He said he could understand how a woman like her could make Rico run late in the mornings. She wondered if Tim would find it equally easy to understand the fact her husband still would not allow her to touch him? Or would he be as perplexed as she was?

Because Rico had done it again. He had seduced her into blind response and successfully deflected her every attempt to explore his body as he explored hers. She couldn't help wondering why and if she didn't believe Rico would see it as the grossest act of betrayal to their privacy, she would ask Tim if there were a physiological reason for Rico's reticence.

Rico slammed back against the rowing machine's resistance and then yanked himself forward with a jerk made powerful by his frustration. He wanted to walk, damn it. He wanted to make love to his wife. Completely. With his whole body.

He'd thought that might be a possibility the night before. His sex had become semierect when he started touching her, but it hadn't lasted and he hated the feeling of sexual helplessness that experience had left him with.

That morning, she'd wanted to discuss their emotions. He didn't know what he felt. He needed her in his life in a way he had not needed Chiara. His inability to experience sexual release underscored that truth. He wondered if his innocent wife realized that. She'd been upset when he hadn't said he loved her, but didn't she realize that what they had was more permanent and lasting than some kind of romantic ideal?

He was committed to her. He knew she was committed to him. In time there would be children. He had begun to hope he would be able to father them in the normal way, but this morning's repeat performance of only a semierection and a temporary one at that, put paid to those thoughts.

He wanted Gianna pregnant with his child. He'd thought consummating their marriage would help her to settle into her role as his wife, but he still sensed a restlessness in her. Once she was pregnant with his child, she would not consider leaving him again.

CHAPTER EIGHT

RICO'S parents arrived back from their anniversary trip late that afternoon to the news of both their son's accident and his first time standing with the parallel bars.

Renata hugged Rico, kissing his cheeks with typical Italian exuberance. "Oh, my son, you are ever the achiever, yes?"

"It was hardly the accomplishment of the century," he dismissed, glaring at Gianna for bringing it up.

She refused to let him make light of it. Besides which his mother's tearful sympathy would have worn thin with him very shortly. Both his parents had been gratifyingly admiring of Rico's choice to help the woman being mugged. Then, not unexpectedly, Renata had gotten emotional at the sight of her son in a wheelchair. Gianna had mentioned Rico's achievement in an effort to focus Renata's attention on the strides he was making, not the results of the accident.

Gianna shifted in the chair she had taken upon entering the drawing room twenty minutes earlier and met his look without flinching. "It is proof positive that you will be walking again soon."

Renata smiled mistily toward Gianna, "Of course Rico will walk again."

Understanding Rico's male pride, Tito said nothing about Gianna's revelation. "Look at how she stands up to him," he commented instead. "No simpering little miss, our Gianna." Rico's father's brown eyes twinkled at her with approving humor.

"*Ay, ay, ay.* I still cannot believe my son had the good sense to marry our girl," Renata responded, going back to sit beside her husband on the sofa facing Rico.

Tito, a commanding man, only a couple of inches shorter than Rico, hugged his wife of over thirty years. "He has good taste like his papa."

Renata blushed, her still beautiful skin taking on a rosy hue. "Oh, you!" She slapped Tito's arm playfully.

Andre's low masculine laugh brought Gianna's gaze around to him. He grinned at his father. "I'd say Rico's taste has certainly improved over six months ago."

Tito nodded, his expressive face showing his agreement. "*Si.* That one. Her heart is as empty as my bank account after your mama went shopping on Corfu."

The others laughed, but Rico scowled. "You imply I showed no discernment in choosing my fiancée."

Gianna stifled a groan. Rico's pride wouldn't allow him to take his family's ribbing in stride.

Andre shrugged. "You showed better taste in selecting a wife, in my opinion."

"We can thank the good God he came to his senses in time," Tito said with tactlessness allowed only in a parent.

"Or maybe the driver of the car?" Renata asked, her expression thoughtful.

Gianna gasped and Rico's scowl had grown worse,

but Renata shook her head, a look of gentle wisdom in her loving eyes. "Things happen for a reason. Rico will heal, but this accident…it has stopped him from making a bad mistake in his marriage." Her expression turned to one of distaste. "He could have been stuck with such a wife! *Ay, ay, ay.* A conceited little miss who took her clothes off for a living!"

Gianna winced and she shot a glance at Rico, her every concern justified by his cold expression.

"Chiara is a model, not a stripper, Mama." Rico's voice dripped icy censure.

Gianna bit her lip. For a man who didn't still love his ex-fiancée, Rico was reacting with singular offense to criticism of her. She tried to tell herself it was just his pride talking. Rico's standards for himself were very high, so high in fact, he found it almost impossible to admit when he was wrong. Even knowing this, his defense of the other woman hurt.

Renata pursed her lips. "In my day, decent Italian girls did not undress for strangers, or parade themselves on a stage in clothing that covered less than their underwear. Can you see Gianna doing such a thing?"

Rico looked at Gianna with enough consideration to imply he was trying to picture it.

She deliberately looked away from those musing silver eyes. She hated the thought he might be comparing her physical attributes with Chiara's. "I'm inches too short and a stone too heavy to even compete for a modeling contract," she said to Renata.

"I don't know. I think you would do things to lingerie Chiara and those other skinny models could never manage," Andre said with a truly wicked intonation. "I've already seen what you do for a bikini." He kissed his fingertips and opened his hand in a gesture of approval.

It was Renata's turn to gasp.

"Andre, it is not appropriate to make such a comment about your sister-in-law."

Andre moved shoulders encased in a well-cut gray Italian suit in a careless gesture. "If I have offended her, I am sorry." He turned devilishly laughing eyes on Gianna. "Have I offended you, *piccola mia?*"

She shook her head, unsure what to say. His comment had embarrassed her, but it hadn't made her angry. She could hardly mind when his expressed sentiments were so good for her feminine ego. Besides, she knew he saw her as more sister than woman and took his remarks in that light. They were the bland teasing of an older brother.

"You have offended me," Rico declared with freezing cool.

"You cannot be serious," Andre taunted. "Had you married Chiara, you would have had to accustom yourself to such comments being made in the newspapers, not just by your brother."

What was Andre trying to accomplish? She couldn't believe he really wanted to bait Rico into losing his temper and yet that event was fast approaching.

"But I did not marry Chiara, did I?" Rico asked, his voice dangerously soft.

"No, and we are grateful," Tito answered for his younger son, doing nothing to lessen Rico's smoldering anger.

Although the subject changed soon after that, the next hour spent bringing Rico's parents up to date about what had happened while they had been on vacation was a tense one for Gianna. She couldn't forget Rico's defense of Chiara, or his angry reaction to criticism of her.

When the conversation moved into business channels, the women excused themselves so Renata could show Gianna the things she'd bought on her trip with Tito.

Gianna ran loving fingers over a hand-embroidered duvet cover. "It's so beautiful. It must have taken a year to finish." The pale lavender silk was covered with purple irises, their dark green stems and leaves intertwined like ivy.

Renata smiled the smile of a woman who has made a killer purchase. "The woman who did it told me it took her several months to finish." She pulled out a white lace mantilla she'd bought off the coast of Spain. "Now this would have been beautiful as a wedding veil."

Gianna felt herself color under the heavy hint. "It's lovely."

"A register office. DiRinaldos do not marry in such cold surroundings. No friends. No priest to bless the union. No gifts." Renata stood up and laid the mantilla over Gianna's hair and settled it around her shoulders, then stood back to admire the effect. "*Si.* This is how you should have looked on your wedding day."

"Rico didn't want to expose himself to the curious stares of wedding guests while he was still forced to use the wheelchair to get around."

"Then he should have waited, that son of mine. To marry without even his parents present..." She shook her head, her disapproval obvious.

Gianna said nothing.

"We will have to plan a proper blessing on the marriage after Rico has regained his mobility."

Gianna made a sound that could be taken as acquiescence and soon Renata was deep in plans for a big Italian wedding which would include everything but the actual ceremony. A formal church blessing would replace it. She shooed Gianna out of the room, saying she had lists to make and thinking to do. Gianna did not point out that as the bride, she should have some say in the preparations. If her own mother were still living, she would be doing exactly as Renata was, only she would have called Renata for advice.

Gianna went to the library and tried to lose herself in a book, but thoughts of the afternoon kept intruding. Although she was horribly relieved that Rico's parents apparently approved of their marriage, she worried that their voiced dislike of Chiara would cause problems with Rico.

Her worry was justified later as she and Rico dressed for dinner. She had gone into the bathroom to change and came out wearing a demure sheath dress in chocolate-brown silk with a gold pendant formed in the shape of a rose and matching earrings she'd inherited from her mother. She'd left her hair down, pulling only some of it back into a gold clip she fastened on the back of her head.

Rico's eyes flared when he saw her and then grew cold.

"Attempting to live up to my parents' image of you as the Madonna bride, *cara?*" His voice was lethally sarcastic and the endearment sounded like an insult.

She looked down at her dress. It wasn't so different than the outfits she'd worn to dinner over the past week at the villa. "I don't know what you mean."

His dark brows rose in mocking disbelief. "Don't you?"

Her fingers curled into her palms until she felt her nails dig into the soft flesh. "No."

"Chiara complained about how you and Andre made her feel unwelcome at the hospital and I dismissed it at the time, but after the visit with my parents and Andre earlier I have to wonder if she saw things more truthfully than I did."

Gianna remembered the accusations. She'd been relieved at the time that Rico hadn't taken the blatant lies seriously. It irked her unbearably that they'd come back to haunt her now, when there were already enough issues in her marriage causing her pain. From the look on his face, Rico wasn't going to believe her version of events, but she had to try anyway.

"Your brother may not be fond of her, but that does not mean he treated her with anything other than courtesy while she was your fiancée. He respects you too much to do otherwise."

"You think so?" Rico had moved until they faced each other with less than a foot separating them.

She swallowed, made nervous by his proximity and the brooding anger emanating from him. "I know it. I was there, remember?"

"*Si.* You were there, but if you aided my brother in dispossessing my fiancée of her place by my side, you would hardly advertise the fact, no?"

Fury filled her. How dare he question her integrity? Chiara was a royal pain in the neck and Gianna refused to submit tamely to an indictment on her character based on the other woman's manipulative games.

"I didn't dispossess anyone because she wasn't there to begin with. When I arrived at the hospital, your fiancée," she said the word sneeringly, "was nowhere to be found. She'd taken a flit while you lay in that bed in a coma despite the fact the doctors had told her having a loved one by your side could make all the difference in your recovering consciousness."

She yanked her hair from his hand, bringing stinging tears to her eyes as the action caused a painful pull on her scalp. "If you don't believe me, ask Andre."

"My brother has made it clear where his affection lies."

"Are you saying you think he would lie to you?"

"For you? Maybe."

"That's ridiculous."

"Is it? My brother has made no secret of his admiration for you."

She looked into his eyes and read anger and something else. "You're jealous," she said on a gasp.

Making a sweeping arc with his hand to indicate the chair, he glared at her. "Is that such a surprise?"

Funnily enough, it was.

"I didn't marry Andre." She'd never wanted to marry Andre. Only Rico. Only ever Rico.

"And yet you found his compliments on your body in a swimsuit pleasing."

"Did you think I should have been offended?"

She didn't know why she bothered to ask. The answer was obvious.

"You should not desire the admiration of other men."

"I don't desire his admiration, but that doesn't mean that when he says something nice I'm going to tell him to stuff it, either. He's my brother now."

"And I am your husband."

How had this crazy conversation gotten started? Oh, right. "Do you really believe I kept Chiara away from you in order to keep you for myself?"

His sensual lips twisted in a grimace. "No. I spoke in anger."

Remembering another time he'd spoken in anger, she smiled. "You were jealous."

He sighed long and loudly, his expression of disgruntlement for once easy to read. *"Si."*

She grinned and did something she'd never done before. She plopped down on his lap and clasped her hands behind his neck, then kissed him on the chin before laying her head against his chest. "Don't be. You have no reason."

His arms came around her in a hug that was almost hurting. Eventually his hold loosened, but kept his arms around her and rubbed the top of her head with his cheek. *"Cara."*

They sat that way for several minutes in complete silence before going down to dinner.

Rico entered his bedroom after two late night international calls to find his wife sleeping, her hand curled under her cheek like a small child. He was still reeling from how much having her sit in his lap voluntarily had meant to him. He had felt like he had his entire world in his arms. The feeling had not been wholly pleasant. It implied a lack of emotional independence he'd never before experienced. Definitely not with Chiara.

He got himself into bed.

His mobility had increased greatly over the past week, but still he could not walk. And things he had always taken for granted were impossible tasks to perform. Like right now. He wanted to pull Gianna across the bed and into his arms. He finally managed it, but only after a lot of maneuvering.

It was worth it to feel her small body curled so trustingly against him. She automatically snuggled into his side, as if they had been sleeping together for years, not a single night. Perhaps in her dreams like his, they had.

Remembering his irrational accusations earlier, he grimaced. Jealousy, he was discovering, could be hell. He'd never been jealous of Chiara. No matter how skimpy the outfit she modeled in. Andre had gotten that right, but just the thought of Gianna in a bikini within fifty feet of another man made Rico see red. He'd ask his mother to find her a modest one piece.

Getting his independent wife to wear it would be something else entirely, he admitted to himself. While in some ways Gianna was traditional Italian to the core, in others she was very American in her thinking and actions.

Her small hand rested against his chest, while one leg insinuated itself over his thigh. He could feel the sensation of her weight, but had to touch her with his hand to experience the softness of her skin. It was maddening.

When would he be whole again?

He let one hand rest possessively over her bottom, keeping her pressed against him in a way that should have caused a certain reaction in his male anatomy, but did not. Would it return with the complete return of his mobility?

The metallic taste of fear accompanied the possibility that it would not. No man wanted to be half a man. He would not let Gianna touch him in case she discovered his lack of true virility. Yet, he ached to allow those small hands to roam over his body in a way he had never wanted Chiara, or any other woman's touch.

One thing was certain. Half a man or a whole one, he would never let her go.

Gianna woke in the morning curled around a pillow scented with Rico's masculine fragrance. She was warm and had the vague impression of being held through the night. Had she been, or was it just wishful thinking on her part?

Rico was the only person at the breakfast table when she went down less than an hour later. She slid into a chair across the table from him. ''Where is everyone else?''

''Papa and Mama are still sleeping and Andre is at a breakfast meeting on behalf of the bank.''

She smiled. ''It's nice to have your parents home.''

His expression of approval warmed her insides. ''They are thrilled to have a new daughter.''

''Renata wasn't happy about how our marriage took place.'' Gianna smiled ruefully. ''Your mother wants to have our marriage blessed. I think Andre was right about her using it as an excuse to have all the trappings of a wedding.''

Rico's smile made her melt inside like milk chocolate on a hot sidewalk. ''She will enjoy it. Do you mind, *cara?*''

''No. When she was making plans yesterday, it made me think of what it would be like if my mother was still alive. It felt nice.''

''Then we will let her have her way.''

She nodded and started eating the fruit she'd served herself from the bowl on the table.

Rico checked his watch. ''Hurry with your breakfast. We have an appointment in an hour's time.''

''An appointment?''

''*Si.* With the fertility specialist,'' he elucidated.

''But why?'' He was weeks, if not days from walking. Why go through IVF if they didn't have to?

''So we can begin the process of making you pregnant with my baby.'' He said it as if speaking to a slow-witted child.

''But…''

''Were you hoping I would forget that side of our bargain?''

Sometimes he could be very paranoid. ''No. I want to have your baby.''

''Then, finish your breakfast so we can be on our way.''

''But, you're almost walking,'' she blurted out.

Something flickered in his silver eyes, but then it was gone. ''There is no guaranteed timeline for that eventuality. I want to begin on a family right away.''

And a baby would be another bond between them, something else to build emotional connections around. ''All right.''

CHAPTER NINE

SHE was still trying to comprehend Rico's desire to try for conception with IVF when they were shown into the doctor's office. The only thing she could think was that he didn't believe he would be capable of fathering her child any other way. She hated the thought of him tormented by such fear, but she knew too little about such matters to assuage those fears.

Maybe she would talk to Tim.

"You realize the more invasive procedure, intravenous fertilization, will not be necessary," the doctor was saying, bringing Gianna's attention back firmly to the matter at hand. "We will be performing TESE on you, Mr. DiRinaldo," the doctor said, talking about the process by which they would collect Rico's sperm, "a fairly painless, outpatient procedure."

Rico nodded, his expression bland.

The doctor turned to her. "You will have to go through intra-uterine insemination, Mrs. DiRinaldo."

Gianna found the ensuing conversation with the doctor embarrassing to say the least. He discussed options and asked questions about her fertility cycle that left her stuttering for answers. She'd never been one of those women who marked things like that on a calendar.

After her third stammering answer, Rico sighed. "Would you prefer I left while you discuss such details with the doctor?"

She felt her face heat with an even stronger blush. "Yes." Her eyes pleaded with him to understand.

His half smile told her that he had. He turned and left the room, closing the door behind him.

The doctor laughed. "I'm surprised he offered to go. Mr. DiRinaldo strikes me as a man who likes to maintain control and his protectiveness toward you is apparent."

But his understanding for her feelings was greater than his need for control, she thought with a warm gratitude. In that, their relationship had grown, at least. He might believe she should not be embarrassed discussing anything with him, but he now apparently accepted that she was.

"What were you saying about the IUI?" She wanted the consultation over so she could get back to Rico.

"The procedure is one of the least complicated treatments for infertility and little cause for concern."

She nodded, encouraging him to continue. The doctor went on to explain what she needed to do to prepare for the procedure and how to keep track of her temperature and other physiological indicators in order to determine the optimum time for the procedure.

Finally, the doctor smiled benevolently. "Although it is a simple procedure, it can be a trifle painful. You understand this, *si?*"

She nodded her affirmative, though she wasn't quite sure why or how it would hurt. Discussing such private matters with two men, even her doctor and husband, held no appeal.

The doctor made a notation in the file open on the

desk in front of him. "You will experience anything from minor discomfort to lingering pain from the procedure. Though to be honest, less than three percent of women undergoing treatment complain of anything more than the most minor of discomfort."

That was comforting, but even with the low percentage…not something she was willing to share with Rico. He might not allow her to undergo the procedure and she wanted his baby. Very much.

"I'm not worried about it," Gianna asserted.

"It often takes as many as six attempts before conception happens," the doctor warned her.

She hoped Rico would have regained full functionality by then, but she nodded in understanding and acceptance.

Rico was called back in and the doctor loaded her down with a lot of paraphernalia that was supposed to let her know when the optimum time for the procedure would occur. She eyed it askance. "I'm supposed to take my temperature every day?"

"Yes. And—"

"Never mind. I'll read the instructions," she hastily inserted before he started explaining the other methods of measuring her productivity in front of Rico. It had been bad enough the first time around with only the doctor in the room.

They left the private clinic after making an appointment for Rico's TESE on the following Tuesday.

It was the day after his appointment when Gianna followed him into the room where he had his physical therapy sessions. Tim had not yet arrived, but Rico settled himself into the rowing machine and started exercising with the same intense concentration he gave everything in his life.

His thigh muscles corded as he forced the machine through its rotation with his arms.

Gianna filled a water bottle and placed it on the mat beside him. "Tim said you took several steps yesterday."

She had gone shopping with Renata and hadn't found out about Rico's progress until Tim and his wife came for dinner. Gianna had been seeing them out, the rest of the family still in the sala, when Tim had mentioned it. He'd tactfully ignored her shock at the news.

The knowledge Rico hadn't shared his progress with her hurt and confused her. She thought they had been growing closer.

"*Si*. Can I expect a big announcement at dinner tonight?"

She flinched at the sarcasm. "Your parents and brother are interested in your progress."

He grimaced. "You are right, *cara*. I should not snap at you. Tell them what you like."

She couldn't help wondering if he were in pain from the procedure the day before. She bit her lip as he continued pushing his body to the limits. "Are you sure you should be going at it quite so hard after yesterday?"

His jaw tensed and he pushed through three more rotations before answering. "I do not need a nursemaid, Gianna."

He hardly ever called her by her first name and she couldn't help feeling it wasn't an indication of intimacy at the moment. "I'm not trying to be one."

"Then why are you here?"

Good question. She'd attended his sessions at first to cajole him into working on his rehabilitation rather than his company. But since their arrival in Italy, he had given more than enough attention to walking again. She continued to come to his sessions to spend time with him because the rest of the day his business kept him occupied. She saw him at dinner, but rarely otherwise.

Half the time she was asleep before he came to bed. Even when she was not, he never wanted to talk. He made love to her, but steadfastly refused to allow her to touch him. She enjoyed sleeping in his arms, but an underlying sense of insecurity accompanied his rejection of her attempts to give back a small measure of the pleasure she enjoyed in his embrace.

She still hadn't worked up the courage to discuss their intimacy with Tim. She wondered if she ever would. Perhaps if she could convince herself it wouldn't be a betrayal of Rico's privacy.

"I thought you liked having me here," she replied quietly, realizing even as she spoke, she'd clearly become surplus to requirements. "I'll leave you to your exercise."

She turned to go.

"Gianna."

"Was there something you needed?" she asked without turning to face him.

Several seconds passed in silence.

"I enjoy your company." Spoken after an uncomfortable pause and in such a stilted voice, she wasn't buying it. Rico was too polite to tell her to get lost, but it was obvious he wanted to. Had probably been wanting to for several days now.

She squared her shoulders and forced a lightness

into her voice she did not feel. "I think I'll find Renata and see if there's anything she wants me to do." At least his mother made her feel welcome, pulling Gianna into her social life and charity work at every opportunity.

"*Cara.*"

"What?" Maybe she'd been wrong. Maybe he would ask her to stay.

"Did you take your temperature this morning?"

The question was like a douse of ice water. The only thing Rico apparently wanted from her was her womb. "No."

"Why?"

"I started." He could figure out for himself what that meant. "I'll be going in for the procedure in less than three weeks if my body follows the normal cycle."

She didn't wait around to hear his reaction. She knew what he wanted. A baby. She was the necessary appendage to the body of his dream. Nothing more. Sometimes, in the night, when he touched her with tenderness that brought tears to her eyes, she convinced herself *she* meant something to him. But she didn't and the sooner she accepted that, the faster she would stop butting her head against the wall of his indifference.

Rico watched Gianna leave and wanted to call her back again, but what could he say? He hated the fact he had to use a sterile medical procedure to impregnate his wife with his child. It made him feel like less of a man. Added to that, having her witness his struggles to return to mobility was becoming more and more difficult. She treated him like an invalid.

She'd gone from cajoling him to work harder to reproaching him for expending too much energy.

The only time he felt like her husband was when he made love to her at night. Then, it made no difference he had less control over his legs than a two-year-old. She responded to him with such passion, he soon became addicted to the sounds of pleasure she made and the feel of her body as she convulsed in release. He found it so gratifying, it was like finding his own satisfaction.

According to Tim, that could very well be the only gratification Rico would ever know again. Asking the therapist about his lack of recovery in that area had been lowering for Rico, but he did not shrink from doing so. He had to know. Tim's comments had been both encouraging and discouraging. In many cases, full capability was restored, but there were the small percentage of men that even after mobility was restored were unable to maintain an erection.

Fear he was one of those men made him short with Gianna. She was his wife, his woman. *He loved her.* He didn't know when the knowledge had seated itself in his brain, but he'd known since waking in his hospital room in New York that he needed her in a way he had never needed another person.

And he wanted nothing more than to be whole for her. Which meant giving his rehabilitation everything he had. Exercising his legs. Going with Tim through the muscular rotations. Trying to walk no matter how many times he fell in humiliating defeat to the exercise mat. It wasn't defeat, though. Not if he didn't give up and with the impetus of becoming whole for Gianna…he never would.

* * *

Gianna saw almost nothing of Rico for the following weeks. She didn't visit him during his therapy sessions and he did not seek her out. He had business meetings during dinner three nights out of seven. The nights he was home for dinner, she kept the conversation centered on his mother's plans to celebrate their wedding.

Gianna avoided any sort of intimate conversation, wanting to sidestep the possibility of rejection. Rico seemed just as intent on avoiding her, coming to bed long after she'd gone to sleep each night. Once, he woke her when he came to bed and she coldly told him she was too tired. She hadn't wanted to deal with the pain and pleasure mixture that accompanied his making love to her. He hadn't tried again.

But there were nights she could have sworn she slept in his arms. He was always gone before she woke and she had to wonder if she had dreamed the sense of warmth and security.

In the middle of the third week, she came out of the bathroom after her shower to find him in their bed. "What are you doing here?"

His brows rose. "I sleep in this bed, no?"

"I meant now. You don't usually come to bed so early."

"So, tonight it is different."

There was something different all right…something about him. Triumph glittered in his silver eyes. Triumph over what? And then it hit her. "Where is your wheelchair?"

"Gone."

"*You're walking?*" she practically shrieked. He'd said nothing.

"After a fashion. I must use a stick, but this is progress, no?"

"Yes!" she shouted and threw herself across the bed to hug him in exuberant joy.

His arms locked around her and she found herself sitting across his lap, her hands locked behind his neck. "You're walking," she whispered with awe. "I knew you could do it!"

"With the right incentive, a man can do anything."

She smiled, her eyes tearing up. "Oh, Rico…" She didn't know what had altered his focus so completely, but whatever it was had her eternal gratitude.

"I thought we could celebrate, no?"

His husky voice brought back memories of their first "celebration" of his progress. A kiss that had irrevocably changed their relationship. Was he thinking the same thing? The sexy gleam of a predator in his eyes said he was. "Yes," she said with a sigh against his lips.

He let her kiss him for several seconds, allowing her to explore his lips with her tongue. It was heavenly. Finally, he was going to let her be an active participant in their loving. She tunneled her fingers into the silky black strands of his hair and deepened the kiss.

He growled against her lips as his hand cupped possessively over her breast. She arched into the touch, joy coursing through her veins from his achievement and this new, more evenhanded lovemaking. She let her hand trail down his neck to his collarbone. She outlined it with one fingertip.

He shuddered under her and she felt feminine power surge through her for the first time. It gave her the confidence to be bolder than she had ever thought possible. She shifted until she was straddling his thighs and placed both hands on the hot skin of his chest. It was her turn to shudder. She had wanted this for so long. The freedom to touch him. She could feel his heart beating a rapid tattoo against one palm and the protrusion of his male nipple against the other.

She wanted to touch him everywhere.

Her hands slid lower and lower as she edged toward that mysterious part of his body, she found so fascinating. She'd never seen a completely naked male in the flesh and she desperately wanted to see Rico. Her husband.

Suddenly his hands gripped her wrists like manacles. "No."

Her eyes flew open and she stared into an immovable gaze of molten metal.

"I want to touch you," she practically begged.

"It is better that I should touch you, *tesoro*."

No. No. No. She wanted this to be equal. "Please."

He ignored her, bending his head to capture her mouth in an incendiary kiss. Her body reacted with its usual mind-numbing pleasure, but a small part of her brain remained functioning. And that part protested this further rejection.

He didn't want her to touch him. He. Did. Not. Want. Her. To. Touch. Him.

The refrain went round and round in her head until it drowned out even the nerve centers clamoring for more pleasure from the hands now roaming over her body.

She tore her lips from his. *"No."*

His eyes opened, a dazed expression in them that almost gave her hope. "Why won't you let me touch you?"

"Is it not enough I give you pleasure, *tesoro?*" he asked in a thickened voice.

Something cracked inside her heart. "No."

"You can say that when your body is already throbbing for release, when you are aching for my touch?" He illustrated his point by gently pinching her nipple, causing her to groan and arch in involuntary desire.

His expression was no longer dazed, if it ever had been. It was calculating and she couldn't stand it. Reasons for their lovemaking when he so clearly did not want her presented themselves to her conscious. None of them were good.

It was all about control. His over her. It renewed his male ego to have a woman so blatantly under his sensual thrall. Then there was pity. He felt sorry for her. It had to be obvious to him that she was in love with him. He'd even said so once. So, he made love to her because he pitied her. Maybe there was even some element of payoff for her willingness to have his baby.

She didn't want to be paid off. She wanted to be loved. A sob welled up and she ripped herself out of his arms, landing on the floor beside the bed. "I want my own room."

He reeled back as if she'd hit him. "What?"

"I don't want to sleep with you anymore."

He threw back the bedcovers, revealing wine-red silk boxers and the hair roughened contours of his legs. "Like hell! You are my wife. You sleep in my bed."

She was so angry, she was shaking. "I'm your incubator," she screamed at him, "not your wife!"

His olive skin turned pale and silver eyes registered shock. "No!"

He reached for her, but she spun away and ran to the bathroom. She slammed and locked the door.

She heard a thump and voluble cursing in Italian. Seconds later, he was pounding on the door. "Come out of there, Gianna."

"No!" Tears streamed down her face. She couldn't stand one more bout of pity sex.

Silence met her defiance. Long moments of utter silence.

"Come out of there, *tesoro.* We need to talk." He spoke calmly, but she didn't feel calm.

"I don't want to."

"Please, Gianna."

She stared at the door as if it might suddenly dissolve and leave her with no defense. "I d-don't want you t-touching me anymore," she said between sobbing breaths.

"Okay. I will not touch you."

"Do you p-promise?" Part of her mind acknowledged she was overreacting, but her emotions were out of control.

"You have my word."

She unlocked the door. He opened it and then leaned against the frame. His expression was almost as tortured as she felt and a white line of stress outlined his firm lips. "I am not a rapist."

She stared at him, appalled chagrin adding to her pain. "I know that."

"Then come to bed, *moglie mia.*"

His wife. Was she his wife? Or was she just his

baby maker? At that moment it really did not matter. Too drained to fight anymore, she silently climbed between the sheets.

He followed her at a slow pace, taking careful steps, his expression one of grim determination. She realized belatedly that the thump she had heard earlier had probably been him falling. Guilt washed over her even as a sense of unreality accompanied it while she watched as her husband walked under his own power for the first time since the accident. Happiness at his accomplishment mitigated some of the pain of his rejection.

He eventually made it to the bed and he slid into place next to her. She reached over and turned out the light.

"Tesoro—"

"I don't want to talk," she slotted in before he could say anything more.

"I need to tell you—"

"No! There's nothing to say. Please. Just let me go to sleep." She started crying again and he pulled her into his arms, cursing under his breath.

She struggled feebly against him, but he just tightened his hold. "Shh, *tesoro.*" He stroked her hair and whispered words of comfort in a mixture of Italian and English.

Her tears finally ceased and he tried to talk to her again, but she begged him to let her be. She would do anything to stave off his explanation of why she wasn't woman enough for a complete intimate relationship with him. Even if he was afraid of an inability to perform, if he wanted her, wouldn't he want to try? Wouldn't he want her help?

A heavy sigh was the only response to her pleas, but his arms remained warm and strong around her throughout the night.

The next morning, Gianna woke up before Rico. Her histrionics of the night before brought a wave of shame. He had wanted to talk to her and she had refused. Stupid, stupid, stupid. But even after her refusal, he had held her and comforted her throughout the night. She loved him so much, but she certainly hadn't let love guide her actions the night before. Well, today would be different.

She absorbed his warmth and allowed herself the luxury of feeling cherished for several minutes before slipping from the sanctuary of his arms and the bed.

Fifteen minutes later, she surveyed the results of her daily tests to measure her body's readiness for the intrauterine insemination. Well, that explained at least part of her irrationality, she thought wryly.

A sound from behind her alerted her to Rico's presence. She turned to face him, her hand gripping the lapels of her robe together at her neck.

He stood framed in the doorway, all six feet four inches of him exposed but for what his silk boxers covered. His hair stood endearingly on end and morning stubble shadowed his jaw, giving him a dangerous air.

Eyes the color of stainless steel surveyed her with intense concentration. "We need to talk, *cara.*"

She nodded and swallowed. Yes, they did, but right now they had things to do. "My body is at optimum temperature for the procedure."

His eyes flared. "What did you say?"

"I need to contact the clinic and make an appointment for today."

"Today?" He looked dazed.

"Yes."

He closed his eyes as if he was battling something mentally.

Had he decided he didn't want her to have his baby after all? "Have you changed your mind?"

His eyes flew open. "I do not know…"

She couldn't believe it. "Does what I want matter at all?"

He looked so grim. "It matters a great deal, *tesoro*."

"I want to try."

His jaw clenched, but his head went up and down in a short affirmative movement.

She called the doctor from the phone beside the bed. Turning to Rico after she hung up, she felt a faint tremor of nerves attack. "He wants me to come in right away. It's better if I don't eat anything first."

"I'll be ready to leave in fifteen minutes."

She stared at him. "You want to come with me?" She hadn't considered that. He'd gone to his procedure alone. She assumed she would be on her own for hers as well.

"*Si.*"

"But there's no need." Did he think she was a basket case after last night? She wouldn't blame him.

"There is every need." The words were implacable, his expression even more so.

She chewed on her bottom lip and nervously pleated the soft velour of her robe. "They're going to put something inside me," she said, her gaze firmly fixed on the plush pale blue carpet.

"And this embarrasses you?"

Give that man a cigar. "Yes."

"I will keep my eyes on your beautiful face, *cara mia*."

That brought her gaze up from the carpet. "I'm not beautiful," she blurted.

"You are the most beautiful woman I have ever known."

"You don't mean that." He couldn't, not unless he loved her. Only love would put her physical attributes above the gorgeous women he had dated.

He grimaced, as if in pain. "I do, but I do not expect you to believe me."

But she wanted to. Oh, how she wanted to. "Rico…"

"Will you allow me to accompany you?"

"Can I stop you?"

Again, the grimace. "In honesty? It is not likely." He said it apologetically, like he was sorry he had his own ideas and intended to follow through on them.

The embarrassment aside, the thought of having him with her was comforting. "You can come. I want you to come."

CHAPTER TEN

SHE realized halfway to the clinic that she'd forgotten to take the prescription-strength pain reliever she'd been instructed to take an hour before the procedure. She quickly swallowed a couple of over the counter meds from the pillbox in her handbag. The dose only called for one, two should make up for the fact it wasn't prescription strength.

Rico was instructed to wait in the waiting room while she undressed and donned an ugly blue hospital gown. She looked down at it ruefully. Somehow it seemed incongruous with an event that was supposed to leave her pregnant with her husband's baby, but then she'd never considered getting pregnant in the sterile environment of an outpatient procedure room, either.

It did not matter, though. She wanted Rico's *bambini,* no matter what she had to do to get them.

Rico was ushered into the room after her vital signs were measured and the nurse confirmed Gianna's morning test results. He smiled as he came in, leaning only slightly on the walking stick.

She smiled back nervously. "Like my new togs?" she asked, indicating the utilitarian gown.

He leaned down and kissed her gently. "I like what is in them better."

His words rendered her speechless with pleasure.

"Did you remember to take your pain medication?" the nurse asked Gianna.

She flushed guiltily and shook her head. "But I took a double dose of the meds I take for period cramping on the way here."

The nurse, a middle aged brunette with a kind smile, patted Gianna reassuringly. "That should be fine."

Rico had tensed beside her at the first mention of pain. "What pain medication? I thought this procedure was pain free. What is going on?"

Gianna reached out and took hold of his arm. "It's just a precaution. Nothing to worry about. The doctor and I discussed this."

He looked unconvinced. "Are you sure? Perhaps we should consider waiting."

"No." She took a deep breath. "This is what I want."

His frown said he wasn't happy about it. He turned to the nurse. "Perhaps she should take some now. Surely you keep a supply for such an occurrence."

The nurse looked doubtful. "We do, but I don't think it would be wise to mix the two medications. Some pain relievers wouldn't be a problem, but…"

She didn't finish her statement, but Gianna got the message. She reached out and took Rico's free hand. "I'll be fine. Please, Rico, don't make such a big deal about it."

Twenty minutes later her grip on Rico's hand was like channel locks around a water pipe and she was bitterly regretting her blithe assurances. The discomfort of having the catheter inserted to her womb hadn't been unbearable, but now she was cramping painfully and the entire lower half of her body felt like it was sharing in the experience.

Tears filled her eyes and she clung more tightly to

Rico, whose eyes reflected the tortures of the rack. He had tried to get her to abandon the procedure at the first sign of her pain, but she had refused. He'd stood by her side willing his own strength onto her. It was a small glimmer of the support she could expect having the baby and even amidst the physical pain, it pleased her.

"Is it almost over?" Rico demanded of the doctor in a voice that implied a negative answer would have a very bad affect on Rico's temper.

"Yes, just another few seconds and we'll be finished."

The man was as good as his word and within minutes everything had been removed. Her hips were elevated with a wedge and the doctor informed her she would have to remain like that for an hour. It would have been fine, if the cramping had stopped, but it hadn't. She didn't say anything, however, already feeling like a wimp for making such a big deal about the procedure.

Rico seemed to know anyway. He didn't say anything, but held her hand and massaged her tummy with a light, gentle circular motion. After a few minutes of the lulling treatment, she slipped into a doze despite the painful cramping.

She was startled when the nurse returned to the room and told her she could change back into her street clothes. Rico had kept up the soothing touch for the entire hour. Normally shy, she made no demur when he showed every sign of staying in the room while she dressed. She found his presence comforting and wasn't about to give it up.

"Is it getting any better?" Rico asked as he helped her into her clothes like a parent with a small child.

She let him zip her dress and settle her braid down her back before she turned to face him. "Yes. Next time, I'll remember to take the prescribed pain relievers, I can tell you." She smiled at him, but he did not return the gesture.

He looked like she'd said something repugnant. "There will not be a next time, *piccola mia.*"

His words left no doubt he meant what he said.

She wanted his baby and was preparing to argue with him, but everything went fuzzy and her head felt like she'd been on a spinning ride at the county fair. She reached out for Rico, her hand colliding with his torso as she felt her knees give way.

She woke on the bed to the sound of Rico shouting. He was chewing the doctor out for everything from her cramping to the state of the world economy. Or at least, that was how it sounded to her still fuzzy brain.

"Rico?" The word came out a whisper, but he spun around midshout, his attention focused in on her with instant probing intensity.

"How do you feel? The pain, is it still there?"

"Only a little bit. I feel kind of woozy."

"I told your husband it is probably the lack of food. We'll give you a glass of juice to bring your blood sugar level up before he takes you home." The doctor's normally calm demeanor appeared a bit frayed around the edges.

She nodded, but Rico scowled.

"If this is so, such a thing should have been attended to before she was instructed to dress. What if she had been alone? She could have hurt herself falling to the floor." His voice rose with every word until he was shouting again.

She winced and touched her hand to her temple.

His jaw tautened. "I am sorry, *tesoro*. You do not need your out-of-control husband shouting right now, no?"

"Did you catch me?" she asked rather than answer his rhetorical question.

"*Si*. It was doubtful for a moment if I could keep us both up, but you are such a tiny thing, *cara mia*. I was able to lift you onto the bed."

A nurse arrived with a glass of apple juice, which Rico took from her with a look that sent the other woman scurrying from the room. He put his arm around Gianna's shoulder, lifting her into a sitting position and placed the glass to her lips.

She drank the juice, cheered by Rico's coddling.

She looked into his metallic gaze as she finished the juice. "You're going to be a wonderful papa."

His features contracted in bleak lines. "Not if it requires a repeat of today."

And if she couldn't have his baby, would he want her still? His actions pointed to an answer she was terrified of believing.

Rico insisted on her going back to bed as soon as they reached the villa. She knew she was supposed to stay horizontal for the rest of the day, to increase chances of conception, but she'd planned on doing so on a couch in the sala. She had not intended being cooped up in the bedroom.

"But I don't want to stay in bed. I can lie down just as easily downstairs," she argued with Rico even as he undressed her and put a nightgown over her head.

"You are in pain. You must rest."

She ground her teeth. "I don't want to."

He smiled, the first lightening of his expression since that morning. "You sound like a recalcitrant child."

"Don't make the mistake of thinking you can treat me like one. I want to go downstairs."

"No, *tesoro*."

"How would you like being bored and cooped up in a bed all day?"

He raised his brows and she felt like shouting. Last night being a rare exception, she never shouted. She glowered at him. "I know you were in the hospital, but you worked. You had your personal assistant around. I visited you. Andre visited you. Even the wicked witch of the west visited you."

"Do you want me to call Chiara and see if she'll pay you a visit?" he asked, showing he knew just exactly who she'd been speaking about. "I hear she's in Milan."

Heard from whom? Had Rico asked? The thought he was still interested in the comings and goings of his ex-fiancée made her angrier. She flounced onto the bed and fluffed her pillows as a backrest with more energy than necessary. "The last person I want to spend the day with is your former fiancée."

"How about me?"

Was he saying he had planned to stick around and visit her?

"*You* kept *me* company in the hospital."

"But I thought you would be going back to work." He'd spent so much time lately at the bank and DiRinaldo industries office, she hardly ever saw him.

"No way am I leaving you alone after your ordeal this morning."

She smiled in receipt of that statement. "Thanks."

"Do not thank me." He picked up the phone, pressing the inside line button. "I'll ring for some food."

She nodded and he spoke into the mouthpiece, ordering a late breakfast for them both. When he hung up, he went to pull a chair over by the bed, but she scooted toward the center, making room for him to sit beside her. "You can sit here if you like."

"I'm not sure that is a good idea."

"Why?"

He made a face. "Having you next to me in bed sends my brain down a path you cannot take at the moment, *cara*."

She thought he was teasing, so she responded in kind. "I'm sure you can control yourself."

"You are only certain of this because you do not understand the workings of a man's mind, I assure you." He sounded so serious, but lowered himself onto the bed beside her, propping his walking stick against the small table with a lamp on it. "How are you feeling?"

"Hungry," she answered honestly.

He smiled. "I too am hungry."

"You could have eaten breakfast," she reminded him.

"Not when you did not."

"Is that some kind of macho guy thing?"

He reached out and brushed her lower lip, making all the air in her lungs freeze between exhaling and inhaling. "It is a Rico DiRinaldo thing."

"You're a pretty special man, aren't you?" Her

lip moved against his finger and it was all she could do not to suck the digit into her mouth. But she wasn't leaving herself open for another physical rejection. Even if maybe she was beginning to understand why he did so, it still hurt.

She pulled her head back and he dropped his hand, an emotion like pain flaring briefly in the silver depths of his eyes.

"I am so special I allowed my wife to undergo a painful procedure rather than face up to my own fears," he evinced in a driven undertone, his head bent the light glinting off the black smoothness of his hair.

She stared at him, flummoxed by what he had said. "I don't understand, *caro*. What fears?"

His head reared back and something powerful burned in his eyes. "You never call me that. You use endearments frequently with Andre, but with me, it is always my name."

She felt like she was walking through the woods early in the morning, when the fog had not yet lifted and she could barely see one step in front of her face. She didn't want to trip on a fallen log and yet felt compelled to take the next step. "Does that bother you?"

"*Si.*" Painfully honest. Painfully vulnerable. Doubly hard for a man of Rico's temperament to admit.

"With Andre, it's natural because they don't mean anything." She wanted to repay Rico's honesty with her own, but it was hard. "With you, they mean too much."

His hand curled around her own. "So, you do not say them."

She swallowed and went for broke. "To me, your name is like an endearment."

He lifted her hand to his lips and kissed the center of her palm. A noise near the doorway heralded the arrival of their breakfast and the discussion was abandoned while they ate.

She yawned when she finished. "I can't think why I'm tired. I shouldn't be. It's not as if I've run a marathon today." He hadn't even let her walk to the car, insisting on pushing her in a wheelchair. She had the sense that if he were just a tad steadier on his feet, he would have carried her.

"It has been a difficult time for you."

"I feel a lot better," she tried to reassure him.

He looked at her for several seconds, as if trying to read her mind, then without a word, he stood up and took the tray to the door and left it in the hallway. He came back toward her, an expression so grave on his features, she felt a physical hurt seeing it.

He did not sit down again, but went to stand at the window, his hand gripping the cane with white-knuckle ferocity. "When I married you, I was not sure I would walk again."

She'd known that—deep in her heart, she had known. If he had believed absolutely in his own recovery, he would never have married someone as ordinary as herself.

"But you believed in me and I needed that." Each word sounded ripped from deep inside him. "I was not thinking about what was best for you and it shames me to admit it."

"You were frightened."

His shoulders stiffened, but he didn't deny it. *"Si."*

"I understand."

He spun around to face her and torment gave his face a haggard look. "Do you? How can you understand me when I do not? I was selfish, *tesoro.* I did not care for your happiness, only my own."

She shook her head, remembering his infinitely tender introduction to lovemaking. "I don't believe that."

"Perhaps you are right. I thought in my arrogance that being married to me, sharing my bed, it would be enough for you."

She had thought so too. It had certainly beaten the alternative...life without him. "I accepted, knowing that was all that was on offer."

"Because you love me and I shamelessly used that love to get what I wanted, what I needed."

"You can't use what is freely given." She didn't want him wallowing in guilt. They couldn't go forward if he was regretting the past.

"Was it freely given?"

She met his gaze, her own steady. The time for hiding behind face saving generalities was over. "Yes."

"You can say that when I seduced you into accepting my marriage proposal, when I took your virginity so you could no longer speak of annulments?"

He really was feeling guilty.

"But I wanted you. I love the way you make me feel when you touch me."

"If that is true, *tesoro,* then what happened last night?"

''You wouldn't let *me* touch *you*.'' And it had hurt so much.

''I was afraid.''

Okay, he'd owned up to being scared when she'd said it, but she never, ever, ever expected those three words to come out of Rico's mouth. ''Why?'' She thought she knew, but she had to be sure.

''I do not know if I can perform as a man.''

''You're afraid I won't turn you on enough to make love to me?'' she asked painfully.

''*Porco miseria!* Where did you get this idea?''

''You said…''

''I said I did not know if I could perform. I said nothing about the beauty and sexiness of your body.''

''But if I were the type of woman you usually went for, wouldn't it be easier on you?''

In her mind, it made sense, but he stared at her as if she'd gone mad. ''You are my type of woman.''

She closed her eyes against the pity she was sure was in his. ''You don't have to say things like that.''

Weight settled next to her on the bed and a fingertip outlined the contours of her face. ''Have you ever known me to lie, *piccola mia?*''

She shook her head, her eyes still tightly shut.

''Then if I say that you are the sexiest woman I have ever known, you will believe me, no?''

At that, her eyes could not remain closed and she opened them to his gently mocking smile. ''You… I…''

''I have never made love to a woman who made me feel more like a man.''

''But you said…''

''That I did not know if I could sustain an erection,

but when I love you, your response gives me joy without my own body's involvement.''

Part of her wished he'd stop tossing the l-word around so flippantly and another, much bigger part of her—her heart—wished he meant it the way she needed him to mean it.

''Have you... Did you... I mean, has there been...''

He laughed huskily. ''If you are asking if I have reacted physically to you, the answer is yes. It did not happen that first time I touched you and this worried me, but I thought when I regained feeling, I would regain this as well.''

She had assumed the same thing. ''Didn't you?''

''I do not know.''

His hands framed her face, his own expression tortured. ''I let you go through the pain today because I, Rico DiRinaldo, was afraid to find out.''

But he hadn't known it would be painful. She'd hidden the possibility from him because instinctively she'd known he wouldn't let her go through with it. ''It's not your fault.''

He shook his head.

''You said you'd had a response.'' She couldn't make herself say the word erection for all her love for him.

''Yes. Many times when I have touched you, I felt a stirring, never more so than last night.''

''But you stopped me.''

''*Si.*''

''Why? I don't understand.''

''If it did not last. If I could not climax...'' His voice drifted into nothingness, but she knew what he meant. He would have been humiliated.

"I would do anything for you."

"*Si*, today you proved this." He dropped his hands from her face and turned away. "I will never forget the sight of you falling to the floor, or the tears in your eyes when they performed the procedure."

"It wasn't your fault," she repeated. "The doctor told me that first day that some women experience lingering pain, but I didn't tell you. Honestly, I thought I wouldn't be one of them and I wanted your baby so much."

"If I had faced my own cowardice, perhaps you would not have felt that sacrifice necessary."

She reached out and turned his face toward her. So typical of Rico to take responsibility for the whole world and its population on his shoulders. "You are not a coward, Rico. You faced your paralysis. You fought it."

"But I did not face my fear and for that you paid."

Incredibly, his eyes glistened. She couldn't stand it anymore. To heck with worrying about if she'd been horizontal long enough for conception to take place. She sat up and threw her arms around his neck. "No, Rico, *no*. I wanted to try for a baby with you. I didn't care how we had to do it. I want to have your *bambini* so much."

He kissed her, softly, sweetly, like a benediction. "How are you feeling?"

"Better."

"No more cramps?"

She shook her head.

"Then maybe we should see if I can give you my child with more pleasure than you felt this morning, no?"

She sucked in air, her heart pounding arythmically. "Are you sure you want to try?"

"Si, mi amore bella."

His beautiful love. If only he meant it. Then she smiled. The tender look in his eyes, his willingness to risk failure...all for her. It was enough.

CHAPTER ELEVEN

Rico's head lowered. His lips brushed hers. Once. Twice. Three times before she whimpered in protest to his teasing.

She turned her head, trying to catch his lips for a more satisfying kiss, but he was busy nibbling his way down her neck.

"Rico, *please.*" She didn't want the gentle touch. She needed more. All of him. All of his passion.

"Shh...*tesoro.*" His tongue dipped into the shell of her ear. "This will be perfect." His voice and sensual touch sent shivers of anticipation and delight cascading along her nerve endings.

Her lips parted on a breathless sound and he finally let his lips settle over hers with firm possession and he took control of the warm recesses of her mouth. The evocative kiss had her moaning and tightening her arms around his neck.

Then she remembered. *She could touch him.* She broke her mouth from his, panting with excitement, but adamant that this time things would be different.

"Take off your clothes, Rico."

He went still. His eyes slid shut and she watched as an internal battle raged within him. Instantly, she doubted her actions. Maybe she should just touch him and worry about getting him naked later. The raw vulnerability on his face hurt her. She was about to tell him to kiss her again, to ignore her demand, when he gently, but firmly removed her hands from around his neck and stood.

"You don't have to—"

He shook his proud head. "I want to. You deserve this. I deserve this. I want to make you mine in the most elemental way a man can possess his woman."

She loved it when he referred to her as his woman. It implied a chosen intimacy, not a marriage of convenience he was stuck with because of his strong sense of integrity.

The removal of his suit jacket acted like a catalyst to her body's response centers and it felt like everything inside her went on hyperalert. The movement of the very air around her became a tantalizing precursor for what was to come.

She watched, enthralled, while long, dark, masculine fingers loosened his tie and pulled it off. He let the patterned silk fall to the carpet with a soft swish of sound. The jet black buttons came next. First those at his cuffs and then the ones down the front of his shirt. One by one, he undid them, revealing the well-muscled contours of his chest in tantalizing bits until the white silk hung open. Black, curling hair made a V pattern on his chest. It disappeared enticingly at the waist of charcoal gray pants that clung to a dauntingly large bulge and the hard, defined muscles of his thighs.

She waited with suspended breath as he shrugged the shirt from his broad shoulders before moving to undo his slacks. He toed his shoes off at the same time he let the pants fall in another crumpled pile of fabric on the floor beside his shirt. He stepped out of them without looking away from her rapt face.

His socks came next and then he stood before her.

Proudly male.

Nude but for the black silk boxers riding low on his hips. He hooked his thumbs in the waistband and she expelled her held breath as he pushed the shorts down his thighs. An unintelligible sound came from her throat as she watched the most intimate of his male flesh come into view.

She swallowed.

She opened her mouth. Nothing came out. She closed it.

She closed her eyes. She opened them again.

She shook her head.

None of it helped.

"Does it get bigger?" she asked in a truly mortifying squeak.

Rumbling laughter had her gaze flying from his incredibly impressive form to his face. He looked amused, darn him. It wasn't funny. How was she supposed to face *that* with any equanimity, she asked herself furiously.

Rico shook his head, unable to believe his wife's reaction. He'd expected concern, perhaps even a little pity. An attack of feminine nerves and genuine fear at the sight of his only semierect flesh had never even made it on the agenda.

She was scared to death of the prospect of his complete arousal and that boosted his morale in a way nothing else could have. She didn't see him as a eunuch. Far from it. By the look on her face, she thought he was too virile. He felt himself stir in reaction and watched in fascination as she blanched. She really was worried, the poor little thing.

And she was little. Over a foot shorter than him and built on delicate lines that made women like his ex-fiancée seem like Amazons. Yet, he had no doubt they would fit together as *il buon Dio* intended. "Your body was created to accommodate mine."

She licked her lower lip, igniting more flames of desire low in his belly. "Are you sure? Maybe, I'm not made right." She chewed that same sexy lip. "I feel full with your finger. I don't think we'll ever get that in."

If he laughed at her, he was dead. He knew it, but still it took all his self-control to bite back the amusement her words invoked in him and the relief.

"You'll stretch, *cara*. Trust me."

He watched as she visibly swallowed and then squared her shoulders as if preparing to face the firing squad. "All right."

He walked slowly to the bed, his bare feet whispering across the carpet. His balance was improving all the time, but he wasn't about to risk falling. She seemed to shrink back into the pillows as he approached, her beautiful emerald eyes wide with apprehension. He stopped when his legs were against the side of the bed.

"Do you want to touch me?"

It was a hard question to ask. He was reacting to her physically already, but still the fear that he would not enjoy the full sexual response he had once been capable of plagued him. If she caressed him and he remained only semi aroused, or worse, lost what hardness he did have, it would be an unspeakable blow to his pride.

But watching her endure pain for his cowardice that morning had made him see becoming whole for her meant taking this risk.

She hadn't answered his question. She simply

stared at him, her gaze seemingly permanently fixed on his manhood. Then her lashes lowered and she shuddered.

"Yes." It was such a quiet whisper, he almost hadn't heard her.

"Maybe it would help, *tesoro,* if you started somewhere else?"

Wide, glistening green eyes, pleaded with him silently.

He reached out and pulled her to her knees on the high, oversize bed. Then he guided her hands to his chest, placing her small palms over the already stimulated flesh of his male nipples. They both shuddered at the contact. She leaned forward and kissed him, flicking a sweet exploring tongue out to taste his skin.

He groaned. "Do it again," he demanded hoarsely.

She obeyed without pause, this time nipping at his flesh with her sharp little teeth. Then her hands began moving. Just as they had the night before, but this time he made no effort to stop them. Small circles over his hardened nipples, fingernails kneading him like a cat. He pulled at her nightgown until she allowed him to slip it off over her head.

Then he pulled her to him, pressing his hard flesh against her yielding softness and they both stilled, their breathing shallow as they absorbed the sensation of body against body. He felt his sex pressed up against the smooth skin of her stomach and it was all he could do not to toss her on her back and impale her. The knowledge he *could* do it flooded his senses as excitement surged through his hardened flesh.

Oh, Mother. He was getting bigger. She could feel

him swelling against her. Her forehead rested against his chest while her fingers dug into the hard wall of muscle in front of her. She'd wanted to touch him, but now that the moment had arrived, she was terrified. What if she did it wrong? What if she turned him off with her clumsy, inexperienced fondling?

Then he was taking the decision out of her hands and putting himself into them. Literally. He pressed his hand over the back of hers and meshing them together, slid them down his torso until they reached the mat of hair at the base of his shaft. It felt silky and springy at the same time. She pressed her fingers into it and his big body trembled, building her confidence. Gently, but with firm purpose, he guided her hand to the rocklike hardness protruding from his body.

"Touch me, *amore*. Touch me, here."

And she curled her fingers around him, awed by the feel of velvetlike skin stretched taut over steel rigidity. She tentatively caressed him from the tip to the base, rejoicing as he made guttural sounds of excitement low in his throat. She wasn't turning him off. His hand closed over hers, forming her fingers more closely to him and showing her a rhythm and a level of pressure that gave him obvious pleasure.

He dropped his hand and she continued to caress him, shocked by the swaying tenseness of his body. She raised her head, taking in the expression of ecstasy on his face, the flushed heat of his skin, the stiffness of his nipples, all bespeaking a level of excitement she had never dreamed she could generate in him.

"You want my touch," she whispered in wonder.

His eyes opened, liquid silver gleaming down at her. "*Si.* Very much."

Tears flooded her eyes. "I thought you didn't," she admitted on a ragged breath.

His body jerked and he pushed her back on the bed, dislodging her hold on him as he settled between her splayed thighs. "I ached for you."

"But—"

He placed his finger over her lips. "Do not talk, *amore.* Feel."

And what she felt. He caressed every inch of her body, first with his hands and then with his mouth. When he buried his lips in the center of her feminine desire, she screeched. "No! Rico... I... You..." Soon her incoherent words turned to moans of the most incandescent delight.

He made love to her with his mouth in a way that sent her orbiting into space almost immediately. She screamed his name as the cataclysm of pleasure burst in her. She writhed under him, the pleasure so great it was almost pain, but he didn't stop and soon his clever tongue was sending her into an oblivion of bliss again.

Pleasure built upon pleasure until it felt like one, prolonged wave. Her body bowed off the bed, every muscle taut with her reaction to his ministrations.

But this time she knew there was more and she wanted it. Needed it. Demanded it with hoarse shouts that would have mortified her if she wasn't so lost to the feelings he gave her. She was shaking with her need by the time he returned to his position above her.

"I want you," she cried.

"*Si.* This I can see." The smug satisfaction in his

voice should have irritated her, but she was beyond irritation at male posturing. He probed her entrance, pushing inside a little bit. "Now we make love."

She stared up at him, sure they could not possibly continue but equally positive she would not pull away. This was too important to him and therefore to her, for her pseudovirginal fears to hold sway.

He smiled down at her, but there was no amusement in his expression. It was the smile of a predator, of primordial man establishing his place in the hierarchy of priorities in his woman's life...at the top.

"You are mine, Gianna. *Always.*"

The mesmerizing intensity in his molten eyes rendered her mute, but she nodded her head. Incredibly she felt her body stretch to accommodate him and then swollen, tender flesh molded around his hardness to leave her feeling completely possessed, filled with him and surrounded by him.

It was more intimate than anything she could have imagined. More emotionally devastating than anything they had done before.

She didn't realize she was crying until he licked the trail of her tears from the corner of her eyes to her temples. "Am I hurting you?" he asked in a shaken voice.

"No." She shook her head frantically, unable to utter another coherent word, but he seemed to understand because he began moving his body.

He slid almost all the way out of her, making her catch at him with her hands, desperate for a return of the feeling of intimate connection. But he did not withdraw, he surged back into her and began a rhythm that quickly escalated to something poundingly hard and fast.

The ecstasy built inside her, making her shout his name and utter other less intelligible noises. How could it be more, better than what he'd already done? She didn't know, but it was. Infinitely more intense. Maybe because they were sharing it. She arched up to meet him, matching his beat, matching his fierceness with her own sensual aggression.

Then the world exploded around her, going black around the edges and she came close to losing consciousness for the second time that day. A scream echoed in her head and she realized vaguely that it had been her own. Then a shout reverberated in her ears as Rico joined her in this ultimate pleasure between a man and a woman, his body bowing, his manhood growing impossibly large inside her.

The tension drained from his body increment by increment until his torso met her own as he allowed his body to settle against her. She hugged him with both her arms and legs, wrapping herself around him in exuberant delight.

"You're a wonderful lover, *caro*."

His body jolted. With a growl, he started raining kisses all over her face. He interspersed them with words of gratitude and extravagant approval. It was all so unreal. Rico, thanking her for making love. Rico, telling her she was the most beautiful woman alive. Rico, kissing her with totally uncool enthusiasm.

He rolled onto his back, taking her with him. She landed astride him, his flesh still firmly embedded in her. She laid her head on his heart and listened to the rapid beat with a sense of the miraculous.

"*Grazie, mi amore bella.*"

She smiled against his chest. "Thank *you*, my love."

His arms tightened around her. "You have restored to me wholeness."

Was that anything like the gift he had just given her?

"I love you," she said, unable to keep the words inside.

"*Si*. With you. This was safe," he said with deep satisfaction. "A man can be vulnerable with a woman who loves him."

She pushed herself up on her arms, causing him to press more deeply into her, and looked into his content face. "I'm glad." Simple, but heartfelt.

"Not as glad as I am." And incredibly she felt a renewed expression of that gladness swell inside her.

She sucked in air on a shocked gasp. "Rico?"

"*Si?*"

"What…" But even as the question was forming, his body was giving her the answer as he arched under her, sending her quivering body on a new voyage of discovery.

He really was intent on letting her share more equally in the loving was her last coherent thought as he taught her to set a pace to bring them both sexual satisfaction.

Gianna woke to the soft caress of lips against her temple. She smiled, her eyes still closed and husky male laughter blanketed her in its warmth.

"*Buona mattina, tesoro.* Open your eyes."

She obeyed him and felt joy well up from the depths of her being. "Good morning." She reached up to wrap her arms around his neck and lifted her face for a kiss, secure in their physical intimacy after a night of making love.

He kissed her, his lips moving over hers with possessive pleasure and soon she was plastered against his shirtfront, her tongue dueling with his. Groaning, he pulled away.

She stared up at him, not comprehending why he had stopped.

"I must go, *tesoro*. I have a meeting this morning. I would cancel it if I could."

Then she noticed the immaculate suit, conservative tie, his perfectly groomed hair and the smooth skin on his jaw from a recent shave. His eyes devoured her with hungry force and she believed he was leaving under duress.

She shifted and winced as her body reminded her just how many times they had made love in the past twenty-four hours.

He brushed her cheek, letting his fingers twine into her hair, which he had unbraided in the most erotic way yesterday afternoon. "Perhaps it is best for you that I go, no?"

She grimaced, but could not deny the twinges of discomfort. "I don't want you to leave," she said regardless.

"I will return as quickly as possible."

She felt her lips curve into a pout and part of her mind was shocked. She'd never pouted in her life.

He gave a groan of male appreciation and nipped at her protruding lip. "I promise."

She caught his mouth for a lingering kiss and then pulled back. "All right. If you promise."

His gorgeous face creased in a smile of sexy approval. "On my life." He kissed her briefly again, as if he couldn't quite make himself leave. "I will cut the meeting short if I can. Take a long, hot bath, *mi moglie.*"

"Will it help?" she asked with projected innocence.

"Si." He stood up, a serious expression passing across his face. "We will talk when I return."

They hadn't done much talking last night. She nodded and smiled.

He moved toward her as if he would kiss her again, but then stopped, a look of grim determination crossing his sculpted features and left. She watched him walk from the room, a sense of foreboding that overshadowed her joy from their lovemaking coming out of nowhere. What did he want to talk about?

Despite the mysterious sense of apprehension, she refused to consider it might be something bad. Rico had spent almost twenty-four hours doing everything in his power to give her pleasure and impregnate her with his child. She should feel a deep sense of security in her marriage, she chided herself.

With that thought firmly in mind, she followed Rico's instruction and had a long spa bath, the water softened and scented with expensive oil that had been a gift from her mother-in-law on one of their many shopping expeditions. The hot, swirling water soaked away the unfamiliar aches in her muscles and feminine flesh.

Later that morning, after a solitary breakfast because the rest of the family was gone from the villa, she was told she had a visitor in the sala. She walked into the room and as it always did, her gaze first went to the rich murals on the ceilings and down one third of the wall. The villa had been in the DiRinaldo family for many generations and boasted artwork by some of Italy's greatest masters.

A sound near the window brought Gianna's gaze around to her visitor.

Chiara stood outlined in the autumn sunlight, her face cast in shadow so Gianna could not read her expression. "I suppose you think you've been very clever," was her opening gambit.

"I don't know what you mean."

Chiara stepped toward Gianna, revealing the look of condescending pity on the other woman's face. "You're a little fool. He won't stay with you now that he is a man again."

How could Chiara know what Rico had only discovered yesterday? He wouldn't have called her. He couldn't have. Gianna's stomach heaved at the thought and she had to breathe slowly and shallowly to stop herself being sick.

"What are you talking about?"

"Don't play the ignorant with me. I know Rico's walking again."

So she didn't know about the other. A shudder of relief shook Gianna. But how had Chiara learned about his walking? Gianna had only found out the day before yesterday. "We always knew Rico would walk again."

"If he'd believed that, he'd never have let me go," Chiara said scathingly.

After his revelation that he *had* had his doubts, Gianna could not bring herself to give Chiara the putdown she deserved. "I don't know what difference you think that makes," was the best she could do.

"You really are a stupid little cow, aren't you?"

Gianna stiffened at the insult. "You clearly have something to say. I suggest you say it and then leave my home."

"Your home? How long do you think that will last? Until you give Rico a baby. That's how long. He knew I wasn't keen on getting pregnant and spoiling my figure. Once you've done your broodmare bit, he'll come back to me, the woman he really loves."

"Rico's not like that." He had far too much integrity to abandon the mother of his child.

Chiara smiled viciously. "When a man wants something enough, he'll sacrifice anything to get it."

"What makes you think he wants you? He let you go."

"He thought he couldn't be the man I needed him to be. He let me go for my sake. Now, we both know differently."

Gianna's hands fisted at her sides and she felt tension filter into every muscle group in her body. Chiara was more right than she knew. Rico's biggest fear, that he would be incapable of making love, not that he would not walk again, had been laid to rest only the day before.

"You don't love him."

Chiara's laugh was ugly. "When you have sex as good as Rico and I had it, you don't need maudlin emotions like love."

Gianna could not bear the image of Rico touching Chiara the way he had touched Gianna, so she forced such imaginings from her mind. "You're very crude and I think it's time you left."

"Not so fast. There are still things I want to say

to you and then I think I'll wait around for Rico to show up. I need to congratulate him on his walking.''

Gianna could not believe the audacity of the other woman. "If you want to see my husband, you'll have to make an appointment with his secretary. You aren't welcome in *my home.*" She emphasized the words, reminding both herself and Chiara that it was she Rico had married.

Chiara's catlike eyes narrowed. "I'm not going anywhere."

"Rico's security staff will say differently, I think."

"You wouldn't kick me out. You haven't got the guts." Chiara sounded shocked and just the tiniest bit unsure of herself as if Gianna's threat had been completely unexpected.

Gianna opened her mouth to answer when she was interrupted by the sound of Rico's voice.

"I didn't realize you planned on company, *cara.*"

Gianna spun to face him, finding his expression maddeningly unreadable. "I didn't. She came uninvited."

"And your wife threatened to have me thrown out." Chiara's voice had gone husky with hurt and much to Gianna's disgust, tears now sparkled in the other woman's feline eyes.

Rico's black brows rose in sardonic question. "Did she really?"

Chiara rushed across the room. Clutching at Rico's jacket with red lacquered nails, she said, "Yes. It isn't enough she's married to you. She wants me out of your life completely."

Rico carefully removed Chiara's clinging hands and turned his silver gaze to Gianna. "Is this true?"

Did he expect her to deny it? "Yes. I told her if she wanted to see you to make an appointment with your secretary. I don't want her in my home."

Gianna wasn't going to put a polite façade on for appearance's sake. Chiara had lied about her in New York, had threatened her marriage just now and Gianna was certain would do anything in her power to seduce Rico back into her bed. She was not a person Gianna was willing to embrace in her circle of friends.

Rico nodded, as if taking in her words. "I don't think an appointment will be necessary, however." He looked down at Chiara, so he missed the spasm of pain that tightened her features that Gianna could not repress. "We can talk now, no?"

Chiara practically purred. "Yes, Rico. Please. I just wanted to see you and tell you how happy I am that you are walking again."

Rico stepped away from her, moving to the drinks cabinet. He poured himself a Scotch. "How did you find out?"

"I met your therapist's wife quite by accident while shopping one day. We struck up a friendship. You couldn't blame me for wanting to keep track of your progress, not after all we were to each other."

The words, the nauseatingly sugar sweet voice and Chiara's obvious duplicity were enough to make Gianna sick. Rico might not have supported her throwing his ex-fiancée from the house, but that didn't mean Gianna had to stand around and watch the other woman work her wiles on her husband.

She spun on her heel and walked out of the room.

Rico called her name, but she ignored him, just as she tried to ignore Chiara's voice telling him to let Gianna go.

CHAPTER TWELVE

GIANNA walked upstairs in a fog of pain. Why had Rico allowed Chiara to stay?

She stopped outside the bedroom door and realized she could not go in. She couldn't face the bed, couldn't face the memories in light of that poisonous woman's threats. She spun around and headed back down the stairs.

She went to the garage and climbed behind the wheel of the first car she found with a key in the ignition. It was a Mercedes sedan. It was bigger than she was used to, but she didn't care. She just had to get away.

The security guard was waving wildly at her to stop when she pulled out of the driveway after pushing the automatic gate opener. Rico and his father had been adamant she and Renata only leave the villa with a security escort, but Gianna wasn't in the mood for company. Any company.

She drove around the city mindlessly until she found herself in the vicinity of the *Duomo*. Memories of Rico bringing her here after her mother's death guided her in bringing the car to a halt. She found parking, which in itself was a shock, and left the car to venture inside the huge cathedral.

She was no longer a child, but she hurt and the vast open space inside the church was just as awe-inspiring to her now as it had been when she was a little girl. She needed the peace she'd found then inside the cavernous structure. Her feet took her of their own volition to the rose windows. Rico had brought her here, to this exact spot. He had told her she could talk to her mother, that even though Mamma was in Heaven, she would hear.

Had she started loving Rico that day?

She hadn't identified it as sexual love until she was fifteen, but Rico had always been the cornerstone to her heart. The only man she could give herself to. The only man she had ever wanted to marry, but he hadn't seen her for dirt. Not until the accident and his beautiful, but excruciatingly selfish fiancée had ditched him.

Gianna leaned against a column, letting her body soak in the sense of peace hundreds of years of pilgrims had felt before her. Rico was hers, but for how long?

After almost twenty-four hours in his bed, she refused to believe he still did not see her for dirt. He'd proven to her over and over again that she was a desirable woman in his eyes.

That didn't mean he loved her, but then again, it certainly did not indicate a lack of feeling, either.

He'd let Chiara stay.

The memory of something he had said the day before intruded with ominous significance. He had said he felt *safe* assessing the level of his virility with her—because she loved him. Did that mean he had only been using her as a testing ground to determine if he could go back to Chiara whole? The very prospect was enough to make her knees buckle and she sagged against the pillar.

But Rico wasn't like that. She knew he wasn't. So, why was she imagining all sorts of ugly scenarios?

"I thought I would find you here, *tesoro*."

Her head snapped up. "What are you doing here?"

His expression was somber. "Looking for my runaway wife."

"I didn't run away." She straightened against the pillar.

"You did not take a bodyguard. You drove yourself off the property, though my security men tried to wave you to a stop."

He made it sound like she'd committed cardinal sin number nineteen. "I wanted to be alone, all right?"

He shook his head, his hair looking black in the muted light of the *Duomo*, his expression bleak. "No, it is not okay."

She glared at him. "You can't dictate my every movement."

"I do not desire this."

Right. "Then why are you here?"

"Because you are here."

"You let Chiara stay in my house," she accused him.

"I had things to say to her."

She angled her head away from him and said nothing.

"Do you not want to know what those things were?"

"No." She didn't want to hear if he still had feelings for his ex-fiancée.

"How can you doubt me after what we shared yesterday and last night?" he asked in a driven tone.

Her head snapped back and she met his glittering,

accusing gaze. "We shared our bodies. According to Chiara, that's nothing new to you."

"We shared our souls and that, *mi moglie*, is something I have never done with another woman."

She wanted to believe him so much. Tears burned her eyes and ached in her throat. She shook her head. *"Si."*

"You married me for all the wrong reasons," she said, fighting to talk around the crying.

His jaw clenched. *"Si."*

The tears fell faster and she turned from him, but she found no peace in her surroundings. There was too much pain slicing through her. A sob welled up and broke past her tightly clenched teeth.

His hands gripped her shoulders. "Do not do this to yourself. The past cannot be changed."

She twisted from him, knocking his hands away. She felt like a wounded animal, wanting to lash out. "Don't touch me."

He spun her back to face him. Pain easily equal to the hurt she was experiencing glittered in his eyes. "Does not forgiveness come with love?"

Forgiveness for what? Did he expect her to forgive him for not loving her? It wasn't that easy, nor was it a matter of forgiveness but learning to accept. "I don't know if I can," she said, speaking to herself rather than him.

She knew she had to learn to live without his love, but she did not know how to do that.

Rico's features set in chilling resolve that even amidst her emotional turmoil made her feel apprehensive. "I will not let you go, *mi moglie*. You are mine."

"I never wanted to be anyone else's." The words came of their own volition, in a pain-filled whisper.

"Then what is this *do not touch me?*"

"I hurt," she admitted.

"Turning from me will not make it better."

Her lower lip trembled and she felt another sob well up.

He cursed and stepped forward. "Come, *cara.* Let me take you home where we can talk in privacy."

She found herself swung high against his chest, his arms unbreakable bonds around her.

"Where is my home?" she asked, thinking of Chiara's smirking face when Gianna had left the sala.

"Where I am." His voice vibrated with purpose and his mouth came down over hers in a bruising kiss.

She responded with a passion released by her anguish. She didn't know how long they stood there, his lips staking claim on her, but eventually the sound of a child asking his mum what the man and his girlfriend were doing penetrated her conscious mind. She pulled her mouth away and it was at that moment, the significance of her position hit her.

"Rico, put me down." The thought of the English tourists watching while she and Rico kissed made her cheeks burn with embarrassment.

Inimical rage burned into her from eyes the color of molten metal. "No."

Why was he so angry? "Think of your legs. It's too much, too soon." What if he fell and hurt himself?

"You are worried about my well-being?" he asked, his ire fading slightly.

"Yes."

"You are not trying to push me away again?"

She sighed, linking her arms around his neck and letting her head fall onto his shoulder. "I can't."

He nodded, the anger completely gone now. She could feel it drain out of him as surely as if it had been herself.

He turned and with amusement and what she could have sworn was masculine pride in his voice, said to the little boy, "She's not my girlfriend. She's my wife."

The child said, "Okay," with the ageless wisdom reserved for the very young while his mother blushed scarlet.

Rico winked and then turned to leave the *Duomo*.

He still hadn't put her down.

"Rico—"

"I told you, I will not let you go."

"I didn't realize you meant it so literally."

"If holding you in my arms is how I keep you with me, then you will spend the next fifty or so years in my constant company." The words should have sounded amusing, but they didn't. They sounded more like a threat from a man perfectly capable and willing to carry it through.

She said nothing else as he carried her out to the limousine waiting in a no-parking zone. The chauffeur opened the door and Rico let her down to get inside. Once they were seated, he pulled her back into his arms and onto his lap.

"What about the car?" They couldn't just leave it.

"Tell Pietro where it is and he will collect it."

So, she told the young security man where she'd parked and handed him the keys, all the while aware of Rico's hard body surrounding her and his hand laying possessively across her thighs.

She looked into his eyes and emotion she was terrified of naming burned in the silver depths.

"Why didn't you kick Chiara out?"

The hand on her thigh moved in a provoking caress. "I did."

"But…"

"She came to our home and dared to upset you, *cara*. I could see it in your beautiful green eyes and the tense way you held your delectable body so erect."

"But…" She didn't understand. "Then why the heck did you let her stay?"

"I needed her to know that I would tolerate no more interference in my life or that of my family, that if she attempted to hurt you again, she would answer to me. I do not play nice, she knows this. She will leave us alone."

"You were warning her off?"

"*Si.* I had barely enough time to make my position clear and have her escorted to the door when Security came with the news my wife had run away."

A twinge of guilt niggled at her. "I didn't."

"You did."

She didn't bother reminding him she had wanted to be alone, to have time to think. The excuse had carried no weight with him at all. "Where do we go from here?"

"Home, *mi moglie*. Back to bed maybe…"

She was tempted to give into the promise in his voice, but she wanted more than a physical satiation of their bodies' desires. "That's not what I meant."

He sighed. "It is up to you."

"What do you mean?"

"I cannot force you to stay if you want to go."

The tight band of his arms around her said otherwise. "And if I don't want to go?"

"I will be the happiest of men."

"You did not love me when we got married."

"You were with me when I came out of coma," he said, she thought apropos to nothing.

"Yes."

"It was your voice, your words that brought me out of it."

She bit her bottom lip. Had it been her voice, her words? "I don't know. Maybe it was just the right time."

"No, *tesoro*. It was not. Do you know how I know this?"

She shook her head, incapable of speech in the face of the warmth emanating from him.

"I remember the words. You told me you loved me."

He could be guessing.

He smiled. "You do not believe me, but it is true. I heard and I woke."

"I could not stand the prospect of a world without you in it." She laid her hand over his heart, even now needing affirmation of the life pulsing in him.

"*Si*. There has been no doubt in my mind of your love for me from the moment I woke. It sustained me, gave me strength when I had little of my own."

"But you don't love me." Even saying the words hurt.

"Do I not?"

"You said you only cared for me."

"And caring, it is not part of love?"

"What are you saying?" Hope was starting to unfurl in her heart like the petals of a rose exposed to the sun.

"How could your love bring me back from a living death if there was no corresponding love in my heart to meet it?"

She shook her head, terrified of believing.

"I did not realize it at first. I tried to stick with the familiar...the safe."

"Chiara."

"*Si*. She wanted nothing from me but my money."

"And your body," she slotted in.

"Without love, it is only that. A body. Any man would do, but for you it is only me, no?"

"Yes."

"Did it never make you wonder when I demanded we marry before leaving New York?"

Of course it had. Nothing about their marriage had made any sense to her. "I didn't understand your wanting to marry me at all, much less so quickly."

"I did not want to risk losing you and I knew you would take your wedding vows seriously, but my reasoning was selfish, *amore*. I wanted you, but was unwilling to admit I loved you. I would have deserved it if you had decided you preferred Andre as I feared."

"You thought I wanted your brother?" Was he blind? She thought Rico's anger toward her time spent with his brother had been possessive pride, not the result of any real fear.

"*Si*."

"But I never even flirted with him."

"He flirted with you." And from the remembered

anger in her husband's eyes, he had liked it even less than she'd thought at the time.

"But you said you didn't love me," she reminded him, hurting a little less, but still not sure what to believe.

"I broke it off with Chiara in New York."

"What?"

"I told her I no longer wanted to marry her. I told her this because my dreams were filled with a tiny green-eyed sprite who nagged me and stood up to me in a way no other woman would dare to do."

"You broke it off with her over me?" She thought it had been his inability to walk. "She said—"

"She convinced herself I had done it for her and that when I started walking again, I would want her back. I didn't. I don't. I only want you, Gianna."

She stared at him, her chest tight with emotion.

His expression was more serious than she'd ever seen it. "I love you."

"You can't," she said, crying again.

"*Mi amore bella*, I can and I do. You are my heart. My life. Without you, nothing matters. I did not tell you of my love because I was afraid. Afraid I would not walk again. Afraid if I did, I would not be able to perform as man—"

"Even if you were paralyzed from the neck down for the rest of your life, you would still be everything a man should be to me," she said stopping his flow of words.

His eyes closed and he shuddered. Then they opened and he kissed her gently. "A man would give his very life for that kind of love, *amore*. It is so beautiful, so real, I thought I could not match it."

"But now you can?" she asked, desperately hoping the answer would be *yes*.

"I realized I could yesterday morning during the IUI. You were hurting and I knew that no matter the sacrifice, I would never allow you to hurt like that again."

She didn't think it was the time to remind him that childbirth wasn't exactly painless. She had the feeling he'd decide to adopt and she wanted to have his *bambini*.

His hands cupped her face and his eyes grew suspiciously bright. "I love you, *tesoro,* with all that I am and ever will be. You are the other half of my soul and I thank *il buon Dio* for that mugger and the driver of the car that hit me because if it had not happened, I would have lost you, the only treasure worth having in my life."

Her heart almost stopped beating. "You can't mean that."

"*Si.* I now understand my mother's views. She knew I would be miserable with Chiara, that my life with you would be superior in every way. What is a little pain, a little work in the face of such a gift as your love?"

She would not have used little to describe the work or pain he'd gone through. "You could have had my love without it."

He wiped at the wetness below her eyes with gentle fingers. "You would have given it yes, but I was not ready to receive it. I was blinded to your beauty and how important you have always been in my life."

She would never agree with him or his mother that the accident was a good thing. It had hurt him too much, but she would not deny the joy his words placed in her heart.

"I love you."

"*Si*. You can never say this too often, *mi amore*."

So she said it again, and again, and again, interspersed with kisses until they reached their home and continued saying it far into the night as he gave the words back to her in both action and voice.

The blessing of their marriage was everything an Italian mother could want it to be. Renata spared no effort in making sure every wedding tradition was observed. This included her daughter-in-law wearing a traditional white gown for the blessing ceremony and the lace mantilla Gianna had tried on the day Rico stood for the first time since the accident.

Doing his part to provide as much authenticity to the occasion as possible, Rico insisted on taking Gianna away for a honeymoon. When they reached the luxury hotel in Switzerland and were once again behind the closed door of their room, she expressed her love for him in the most intimate way she could.

Remembering his fascination with her hair, she unbound it and used it like he had taught her, painting his body with erotic strokes, eventually driving him to a passionate, almost bruising possession. Afterward, they lay entwined whispering words of love in Italian and English.

"My baby, it is here. I feel it." Rico laid his big hand over her stomach.

She smiled mistily. "I do, too."

"I love you, *tesoro*."

"No more than I love you, *caro*."

* * *

Eight months later, they were proved right when she gave birth to paternal twins. Rico was convinced he was so potent for her that both the IUI procedure *and* their making love had borne fruit. Who was she to doubt him?

Her love had brought him back from a living death, why couldn't his love conceive life not once, but twice in her womb?

The world's bestselling romance series.

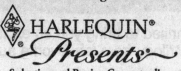

Seduction and Passion Guaranteed!

THEPRINCESSBRIDES

For duty, for money…for passion!

Discover a thrilling new trilogy from a rising star of Harlequin Presents®, Jane Porter!

Meet the Royals…

Chantal, Nicolette and Joelle are members of the blue-blooded Ducasse family. Step inside their sophisticated and glamorous world and watch as these beautiful princesses find they have to marry three international playboys—for duty, for money… and definitely for passion!

Don't miss

THE SULTAN'S BOUGHT BRIDE (#2418)
September 2004

THE GREEK'S ROYAL MISTRESS (#2424)
October 2004

THE ITALIAN'S VIRGIN PRINCESS (#2430)
November 2004

Pick up a Harlequin Presents® novel and you will enter a world of spine-tingling passion and provocative, tantalizing romance!

Available wherever Harlequin books are sold.

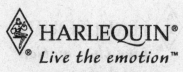

Live the emotion™

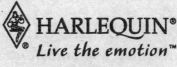

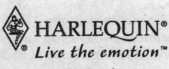

If you enjoyed what you just read,
then we've got an offer you can't resist!

Take 2 bestselling
love stories FREE!
Plus get a FREE surprise gift!

Clip this page and mail it to Harlequin Reader Service®

IN U.S.A.	IN CANADA
3010 Walden Ave.	P.O. Box 609
P.O. Box 1867	Fort Erie, Ontario
Buffalo, N.Y. 14240-1867	L2A 5X3

YES! Please send me 2 free Harlequin Presents® novels and my free surprise gift. After receiving them, if I don't wish to receive anymore, I can return the shipping statement marked cancel. If I don't cancel, I will receive 6 brand-new novels every month, before they're available in stores! In the U.S.A., bill me at the bargain price of $3.80 plus 25¢ shipping & handling per book and applicable sales tax, if any*. In Canada, bill me at the bargain price of $4.47 plus 25¢ shipping & handling per book and applicable taxes**. That's the complete price and a savings of at least 10% off the cover prices—what a great deal! I understand that accepting the 2 free books and gift places me under no obligation ever to buy any books. I can always return a shipment and cancel at any time. Even if I never buy another book from Harlequin, the 2 free books and gift are mine to keep forever.

106 HDN DZ7Y
306 HDN DZ7Z

Name	(PLEASE PRINT)	
Address	Apt.#	
City	State/Prov.	Zip/Postal Code

* Terms and prices subject to change without notice. Sales tax applicable in N.Y.
** Canadian residents will be charged applicable provincial taxes and GST.
  All orders subject to approval. Offer limited to one per household and not valid to
  current Harlequin Presents® subscribers.
  ® are registered trademarks owned and used by the trademark owner and or its licensee.

PRES04   ©2004 Harlequin Enterprises Limited

like a phantom in the night comes
a new promotion from

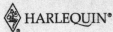 **HARLEQUIN®**

INTRIGUE®

GOTHIC ROMANCE

Beginning in August 2004, we offer you
a classic blend of chilling suspense and
electrifying romance, starting with....

A DANGEROUS INHERITANCE
LEONA KARR

And don't miss a spine-tingling Eclipse tale each month!

September 2004
MIDNIGHT ISLAND SANCTUARY
SUSAN PETERSON

October 2004
THE LEGACY OF CROFT CASTLE
JEAN BARRETT

November 2004
THE MAN FROM FALCON RIDGE
RITA HERRON

December 2004
EDEN'S SHADOW
JENNA RYAN

Available wherever Harlequin books are sold.
www.eHarlequin.com

HIECLIPSE